CONFESSIONS OF A TEENAGE DRAMA QUEEN

CONFESSIONS OF A TEENAGE DRAMA QUEEN

DYAN SHELDON

CANDLEWICK PRESS
CAMBRIDGE, MASSACHUSETTS

Copyright © 1999 by Dyan Sheldon

Second paperback edition in this format 2005

Library of Congress Cataloging-in-Publication Data

Confessions of a teenage drama queen / Dyan Sheldon. —1st ed.
p.   cm.
Summary: In her first year at a suburban New Jersey high school, Mary Elizabeth Cep, who calls herself "Lola," sets her sights on the lead in the annual drama production and finds herself in conflict with the most popular girl in school.
ISBN-10 0-7636-0822-X (hardcover)
ISBN-13 978-0-7636-0822-4 (hardcover)
[1. Identity—Fiction. 2. Interpersonal relations—Fiction.
3. High schools—Fiction. 4. Schools—Fiction.] I. Title
PZ7.S54144Co   1999
[Fic]—dc21   98-53914

2 4 6 8 10 9 7 5 3

ISBN-10 0-7636-1848-9 (paperback)
ISBN-13 978-0-7636-1848-3 (paperback)
ISBN-10 0-7636-2416-0 (reformatted paperback)
ISBN-13 978-0-7636-2416-3 (reformatted paperback)
ISBN-10 0-7636-2827-1 (second trade paperback format)
ISBN-13 978-0-7636-2827-7 (second trade paperback format)

Printed in the United States of America

This book was typeset in Amasis MT.

Candlewick Press
2067 Massachusetts Avenue
Cambridge, Massachusetts 02140

visit us at www.candlewick.com

For Kathy, Mary, and Patty

1

MY YOUNG LIFE AND HARD TIMES

It is a sad and shocking fact of my young life that my parents named me Mary Elizabeth Cep by mistake. I've known since I was five that my true name is Lola. I don't remember where I first heard it, but I loved it immediately. *Lola.* . . . Lola is romantic and mysterious. It's evocative and resonant. It's unusual—as I am. Mary Elizabeth sounds like the maid in an English drama. You know, "Mary Elizabeth," smarms the Lady of the Manor, "please show Mr. Smudgins into the parlor." Having a generous nature, I can forgive my parents this error, major though it is. I can see that it wasn't really their fault. They both watch PBS a lot. But that doesn't mean that I have to accept their mistake as final.

When I become an actor, I'm going to legally change my name to Lola Elspeth Cep. Or maybe Lola Elspeth Sep. I haven't made up my mind about the spelling yet.

My family, naturally, has always stubbornly refused to call me Lola.

"Mary's the name on your birth certificate," says my mother, "and that's the name we're using."

My close relatives are astoundingly unimaginative,

especially considering that we share a common gene pool. But then, another of the more shocking truths of my young life is that no one in my family truly understands me. They seem to think I'm going through a stage, although even my mother admits that this stage has been lasting a pretty long time. Like since I was born. Whenever I announce what I'm going to do when I become an actor, my mother always laughs and says, "What do you mean, *when*?"

She calls me the Drama Queen, though not to my face. Sometimes I hear her on the phone to my dad or her parents. "Oh, the Drama Queen?" she'll say. "This week she seems to be in an Edward Albee play." The twins must hear her, too, because sometimes they do call me Drama Queen to my face. Not that I'm blaming my siblings for their limitations. Pam and Paula are only eight, and, like our mother, they're hopelessly ordinary. Since we have different fathers, I can only assume that my uniqueness is due to some latent gene in the Ceps that skipped about twenty generations till it finally emerged in me. In my family, I'm like a flamingo in a flock of pigeons. Expecting them to understand would be like expecting a cat to understand *Hamlet*. I mean, really . . . do tortilla chips fly? Is the moon made of cheese?

Anyway, we used to live in New York City, in this great old building on the Upper West Side, but last year my mother moved us to a ranch house in the soporific suburb of Dellwood (or as I affectionately call it,

2

Deadwood), New Jersey. New Jersey! At first I thought she must be joking. After I was forced to accept that my mother was grotesquely serious, I consoled myself with the fact that at least she wasn't moving us to Nebraska. You can't even visit New York from Nebraska.

Like most truly creative people, I loathe the suburbs. Living in the suburbs is like being dead, only with cable TV and pizza delivery. In New York, you live with your finger on the cultural pulse of the universe. Plays, operas, dance, books, music, films, artists— everything's there and happening. People in New York get excited when there's a new exhibition at the Met or if Scorsese's filming in Brooklyn. In the suburbs, people get excited when they have their kitchens redone.

And besides the constant intellectual and spiritual stimulation of the greatest city in the world, there are always a zillion things going on in New York, and tons of famous people around. You may not believe this, but I once bumped into Johnny Depp in the East Village. He was coming out of a restaurant, and I didn't see him because I had these really dark sunglasses on and they more or less made me legally blind. Usually, though, if I wanted to meet an actor I'd find out where they were shooting a movie. I met Robert De Niro, Robin Williams, Al Pacino, and Michelle Pfeiffer like that. I got all their autographs.

My mother says that living in The City is like living on a movie set, not like living in a real town. That's one of the reasons we moved, so we could live in a real town—for the sake of the twins. The only things they ever shoot in Dellwood are home videos and the occasional rabbit. The only reason Johnny Depp would be coming out of a restaurant in Dellwood is if his car broke down while he was on his way somewhere else and he had a cup of coffee while he was waiting for it to be fixed. As far as living in Dellwood is concerned, I'm like a bird in a cage with a good school district.

I understood my mother's concern about Pam and Paula, of course—they were only seven at the time we moved, which is a very impressionable age—but I couldn't see why my mother wouldn't let me stay behind in The City. I could have lived with my dad; he has a spare room. And he lives in the East Village, which is the coolest place in Manhattan, if not in the entire universe. I know I could have talked him into it—he's a lot more malleable than his former wife—but my mother wouldn't hear of it. She has custody, and she's keeping it. Though that isn't exactly how she put it. "Your father and I have our differences, but even he doesn't deserve *that*," was what she said.

But I have a positive nature. I believe in making the best of even the worst situation. I mean, you have to, don't you? There's no point being negative about things you can't change—you only make them worse. And anyway, as I always say, every cloud has a solid gold lining.

The solid gold lining in the black thundercloud of moving to Deadwood was that it gave me a chance to re-create myself a little, as all great actors do. Back in The City, at least half the kids I went to school with were kids I'd gone to school with most of my life. They called me Mary. They looked at me and saw the little girl who threw up at Edna Rimbaud's seventh birthday party. They knew all the dull and embarrassing details of my existence. It was like playing Peter Pan for eleven years. To the audience, you're this little boy in a green leotard, and that's it. You'll still be Peter Pan when you're fifty, while lesser actors get to play King Lear.

Dellwood, however, was an empty stage as far as I was concerned. An empty stage to which I was allowed to bring my own script. I didn't have to go gently into the good suburban night. I could choose whatever role I wanted—be whatever I wanted to be—and no one would know any better. No one who wasn't related to me would ever call me Mary again.

Looked at in that way, the move to Deadwood was almost exciting. It was definitely a challenge. The life without challenge is a life without depth.

There was another way to look at it, too. Besides raging against the dying of the lights of The City from my life, I now had the opportunity to bring one of those lights with me into the wilderness. Myself. Lola Elspeth Cep (or Sep). I would be a beacon for all the confused youth of Dellwood who needed reassurance that there was more to living than beer parties and shopping. I would be a source of nourishment to those starving, embryonic souls who were looking for true passion and meaning in their humdrum lives. At last I could start to be the great actor Lola Cep.

A legend was about to be born.

I think it's safe to say that no one at Deadwood High—student body and staff alike—had ever seen anyone quite like me. And this, of course, was to my advantage. They didn't know what to expect. My first few weeks were devoted to showing them what to expect: the unexpected; the unusual; the individual; the unique. One week I'd dress only in black; the next my colors would be vibrant and bright. One week I'd be quiet and remote; the next I'd be gregarious and funny. It was a demanding part, but it took my mind off other things.

Like how difficult it was to be a beacon in the subterranean, windswept, and coal-black abyss that is Dellwood, New Jersey.

I had no trouble getting everybody at school to call me Lola. I told my teachers that even though the register said my name was Mary, Lola was what I'd been called at home since I was a squalling infant in my mother's arms.

Only Mrs. Baggoli, my English teacher, put up a struggle.

"Lola?" Mrs. Baggoli stared at me with her gimlet

eyes. "You want to be called Lola?"

Ignoring the soft snickers around me, I nodded. "My parents fell in love watching *Damn Yankees* together," I explained, inspired. "That's why they call me Lola." As far as I know, neither of my parents has ever seen *Damn Yankees*. I saw it by chance when I was home with the flu one winter. I would have turned it off if one of the characters weren't named Lola. One of the few signs that my parents are actually intelligent enough to be related to me is the fact that they both detest musicals. But Mrs. Baggoli believed me.

"'Whatever Lola wants, Lola gets'?" queried Mrs. Baggoli.

I'd known she'd catch the reference. She was the drama coach as well.

I smiled. It was a good-natured, self-mocking smile. Teachers hate any sign of arrogance.

"I was two when they started using it," I said. "You know what two-year-olds are like."

"Don't I just," said Mrs. Baggoli, with what I took as a significant look at the rest of the class. "All right, Lola," she went on, penciling my real name in her register. "I'll try to remember."

As I've already said, however, I was less successful in other areas. I'd pretty much thought that all I had to do was appear on campus like an incredible sunset after a gray, dreary day, and the starving young souls of Dellwood would immediately abandon their videos and glossy magazines and flock to me, begging for shelter from the storm of meaningless trivia that made up their lives.

But I was wrong. The youth of Dellwood probably wouldn't have noticed a nuclear explosion, never mind a messenger of hope from the greater world. In my first year in the clean air and safe streets of Dellwood (two more of my mother's reasons for moving), I've met only one truly kindred spirit. That's my best friend, Ella Gerard.

There was nothing about Ella to suggest that here was my spiritual kin the first time I saw her. She looked like most of the other girls in my homeroom—expensively if dully clothed, well-fed, perfectly groomed, their teeth gleaming and their hair bouncing because they use the right toothpaste and shampoo. If New York is a kettle of soup, where tons of different spices and vegetables float around together, all part of the whole but all different at the same time, then Deadwood is more like a glass of homogenized milk. Ella was wearing a non-descript pink A-line dress, and white and pink sneakers. The kindest thing you could say about her hair—which was twisted into a tight ball at the back of her head— was that it existed. Although Ella shops in the same stores as most of her classmates, she always goes for what Mrs. Gerard calls "the classic look," which means that everyone else dresses like the followers of fashion that they are, and Ella dresses like her mother.

That first morning, I sat at the front of the room in my genuine U.S. Army fatigues, dyed purple by my own fair hands, and the Che Guevara T-shirt my dad brought me back from Mexico, listening to the other girls catch up on the summer gossip and sort out who was seeing whom and who was wearing what and when the first big fall party was going to be, feeling like a visitor from Alpha Centauri. A visitor from Alpha Centauri who was wishing she'd stayed at home. I could tell that every morning I would sit there, ignored by the other girls, hearing practically the same conversations over and over again. And I could also tell that every morning I would sit there, and they would make a show of checking me out and then looking at each other, smirking at the way I was dressed because they themselves were walking billboards, advertising whatever was in fashion that week, ignorant of true style and flair. The girls in Deadwood get their fashion ideas from *Seventeen* and television. They don't wear clothes as a statement of their inner selves, as I do; they wear labels.

Anyway, Ella sat near me in homeroom. The kids in Dellwood not only dress the same and talk the same; when they think, they pretty much think the same, too. But I sensed almost immediately that Ella was different in that last, crucial respect.

Carla Santini (more on her later . . .) was the center of all meaningful homeroom conversation among the girls. Sophisticated, beautiful, and radiating confidence the way a towering inferno radiates heat, she swept into the

9

room in black pants and a short black sweater as though she'd just stepped from the pages of *Vogue*. Although she'd checked me out the second her foot was through the door, it was a good five minutes before she finally deigned to talk to me.

"Aren't you the girl who just moved into the old Swenska house?" she asked. She was using the sickeningly charming voice I've come to know so well, but she still managed to emphasize the word *old* and make it sound as though it meant more than "no longer young."

Taking their cue from Carla Santini, her entourage all looked at me, too. They were barely breathing.

"Maybe," I said, returning her sugar-overdose smile with one of my own. I'd checked her out, too, without even seeming to look her way. I'd known girls like Carla Santini before—there are lots of girls in New York who think the world wasn't complete until they were born—and I'd never liked one of them. "I didn't realize our house had a name."

The boy behind me, Sam Creek (more on him later, as well), snorted. I saw Ella's mouth tremble.

Carla Santini's laughter rang through the classroom like an alarm.

"Is that supposed to be the famous New York sense of humor?" she asked. Loudly.

That caught the attention of the few people who weren't already riveted by the spectacle of Carla Santini putting me through my paces.

"Are *you* from the city?" asked Carla Santini's

sidekick, Alma Vitters (more on her later, too). She made it sound like she was saying, "You mean, *you're* from Alpha Centauri?"

Before I could say, proudly, that I certainly was from The City, Carla answered for me.

"That's right," she said. "A real city slicker." She gave me a phony look of sympathy. "You must find it pretty dull in Dellwood, after New York," purred Carla.

"You won't for long with her around," whispered a voice in my ear. I glanced right. Sam Creek was leaning forward on his arms as though falling asleep.

By then I'd figured out who Carla Santini was. Her mother was the real estate agent who sold my mother the old Swenska house. It was obvious that, despite Carla's show of innocent curiosity, she already knew a lot about me and my family. Everything her mother knew: our income, our lack of a male parent, probably even the fact that I hadn't wanted to move.

"I don't know yet." I smiled that famous New York choke-yourself smile. "I only just got here."

Carla rang a few more alarms.

"Seriously," she said when she was finished being incredibly amused. "Dellwood must be a big change. I mean, New York . . ."

It was at this point that other people began to join the conversation. Someone told a story about her aunt being mugged not five minutes after she got off the train at Penn Station. One of the boys claimed to know the statistics of violent deaths in The City for the last five years. One of the girls told a story about her friend's friend who was abducted off the street in New York in broad daylight in front of dozens of people, and no one tried to help her. Someone else said he'd seen a documentary about gangs that made him turn down free tickets to a Knicks game at Madison Square Garden.

"Well, my parents took me to New York for my birthday last year," said Ella, "and I thought it was beautiful." She smiled. It wasn't a big smile, but it was a sincere one. Which made a nice change. "You know," she continued, "the lights at night and everything? I felt like I was visiting Oz."

That was when I knew that despite her straight and rather uninspired appearance, inside Ella Gerard was a free spirit waiting—no, begging—to be released. I recognized her as the sister of my soul, who, unlike Pam and Paula, the sisters of my flesh, had everything important in common with me.

"You should see it at Christmas," I said. "Fifth Avenue at Christmas is better than Oz. It's like walking through the Milky Way."

Carla Santini's laugh this time was less like an alarm and more like a flak attack.

"Except that nobody's going to rape or murder you in the Milky Way," said Carla.

The cackling only stopped because Mr. Finbar, our homeroom teacher, stumbled in just then and told us all to shut up.

Ella is shy and she's quiet, but she's kind and has a good sense of humor. We were in all the same classes last spring except math (Ella was in the advanced math class, but the creative mind can have a difficult time with mathematics, so I wasn't), and when she discovered that we had almost identical schedules, she dedicated herself to showing me around. I knew that, subconsciously, Ella wanted to be friends because she was attracted to my style and originality, but I acted like she was the one who was doing *me* the favor.

We had bonded forever by the end of the day.

It took longer than I'd anticipated, but I finally made Deadwood High recognize my true potential. There are people—like my parents and Mrs. Baggoli—who look at what happened another way, of course, as doubters and scoffers always will. My mother said I was lucky. My father said I was lucky. The cops said I was lucky but also brave. Mrs. Baggoli said that I never cease to amaze her.

It was Mrs. Baggoli's idea that I write about what happened in my own "inimitable style" for my final English project.

"Perhaps if you put it down on paper, you'll see things a little more objectively," Mrs. Baggoli suggested. She sighed. "Try very hard to stick to the facts, Lola. Don't embellish too much."

"I don't," I said. "I always try to be as objective as a person can be."

Mrs. Baggoli sighed again. "Well, try a little harder."

So I'm trying really hard to make sure that the real truth is told. And this is the real truth. Everything I'm about to tell you occurred exactly as I say. And I don't mean just the everyday, boring things about school, and my family, and stuff like that. I mean *everything*. Even the things that seem so incredible, so totally out of this solar system, that you think I must have made them up—they're true, too. And nothing's been exaggerated. Not the teensiest, tiniest, most sub-atomic bit. It all happened exactly as I'm telling it.

This is my story.

It starts with the end of the world.

2

THE WORLD ENDS

The world ended on the fifth of March at exactly 11:13 P.M., give or take a second or two.

It started out as just a regular day. In a play, you know something terrible's about to happen because the weather's so bad, or you run into a few witches on your way home. But not even the weather was giving any clues that day. It was cold but bright and sunny, and there wasn't a witch in sight, unless you count Carla Santini.

I was in a *Gone With the Wind* kind of mood when I got up that morning, so I wore the black velvet cape I'd just bought in a local thrift store. In the afternoon, Ella and I went to her house. We usually go to her house because she's an only child and, consequently, is allowed to live her life in peace and privacy, unlike some of us who were less fortunate in our choice of parents.

Mr. and Mrs. Gerard have always been polite and pleasant to me, but I don't kid myself that means they like me. They don't like me. They're just always polite and pleasant, period. They never yell or are sarcastic, like some people's parents. They never have bad moods, and they never fight with each other. They're always giving each other quick cheek smooches and calling each other "darling" and "honey." They remind me of parents in a corn-flake commercial. You know, perfect and always pleasant and reasonable, even when the box is empty.

Ella's house is always clean and neat, and most of the furniture is covered in plastic. There are never any shoes under the coffee table or empty cups left by the side of the couch. You never have to wipe the TV off with your sleeve so you can see the picture. Ella's house is so frightfully immaculate that it looks more like a model home than a real house. I'm afraid to touch anything; which is just as well, because I can tell from the way Mrs. Gerard usually watches me (closely and with a stiff smile) that she's afraid, too.

That afternoon I caught Mrs. Gerard looking at me as she put the snack she'd made us on the table. In my house, though my mother will occasionally stretch to tossing you a bag of potato chips or pretzels, the only way a person usually gets fed is if she feeds herself (and then she usually has to feed everybody else as well), but not in Ella's house. Mrs. Gerard is a professional mother. She not only does three meals a day; she also does everything in between. That afternoon she made us grilled cheese sandwiches and microwaved French fries. She used two different kinds of cheese, and she cut each sandwich in quarters and garnished it with a sprig of parsley.

"Wow," I said, "this is just like eating in a diner."

Ella choked back a giggle.

That was when I caught Mrs. Gerard looking at me. I'd seen that look before. Kind of awestruck but worried, as though she'd just realized I was related to Edward Scissorhands and couldn't touch anything without cutting it into shreds.

When she saw that I was watching her with a contemplative look of my own, Mrs. Gerard laughed. Hers is a laugh that makes me nervous. It doesn't sound happy, like a laugh should; it sounds as though she couldn't think of anything else to say or do.

"Surely you have grilled cheese sandwiches at home," said Mrs. Gerard. You could hear the rest of her sentence kind of dangling in the air: *don't you?*

Mrs. Gerard is always curious about what I do "at home." You'd think she was taking a course in sociology instead of advanced cooking.

I nodded. "Oh, sure, only they're usually burnt because all we have is this sandwich toaster you put on the stove, and we never have parsley with them." My mother's idea of a garnish is a napkin.

"No microwave?" Mrs. Gerard laughed again. "I thought everyone had a microwave these days."

As far as I can tell, Mrs. Gerard also thinks that everyone has a housekeeper, a gold American Express card, and limitless time to make sure there are no water marks on the glasses.

"We don't." I bit into my sandwich. It was delicious. "My mother doesn't approve of them."

I hadn't meant to say that last part; it just kind of came out. Mrs. Gerard's even more curious about my mother than she is about what I do at home. Mrs. Gerard can't get over the fact that Karen Kapok and I have different last names, *and* she's never before met a woman who has biceps like Schwarzenegger and is always covered in clay.

Mrs. Gerard arched one impeccable eyebrow.

"Doesn't *approve* of them?" She rattled out a little more nervous laughter. "I've never heard of anyone taking a moral stance on an appliance before."

Mrs. Gerard had never before cracked a joke in my presence. Since Mr. Gerard works fourteen hours a day and is almost never seen by me, he hadn't either, but I'd always assumed that Ella's sense of humor must come from him. This was the first time it seemed like I might be wrong about that. I laughed, too, enthusiastic and encouraging.

Mrs. Gerard, however, had stopped laughing.

"Are you serious?" she asked. "Your mother really doesn't approve of microwaves?" You'd think I'd said she didn't approve of breathing.

I decided not to get into this discussion. If Ella's mother pressed me on what things my mother did and did not approve of, we could have been there till morning.

"She has very strong opinions," I said, vaguely. I took another bite. "It's because she's Polish."

There's no food allowed in the Gerard bedrooms because of Mrs. Gerard's fear of attracting insects, so after we had eaten, Ella and I went to her room to listen to the new Sidhartha CD again. We knew most of the songs by heart even though we'd only had it two days. Ella likes Sidhartha's first album better, but I think this one is more profound and emotionally powerful. Their other albums make me think, but this one really engulfs my soul. When Stu Wolff (the band's creative heart) sings, "There's something in me that always wants more . . . more moons and stars and music in the wind . . . ," it's as though he's talking just to me.

Sidhartha, if you haven't guessed, is our absolute favorite band. I'd been lobbying my mother for months to let me see them the next time they played in The City, but not with a lot of success. My mother said she'd see—which meant I had a chance if I handled her right—but Ella wouldn't even ask her parents because it would upset them and make them worry about her. Mr. and Mrs. Gerard are actively terrified of young men with black leather and tattoos. They tolerate her love of Sidhartha, but warily. You can tell that they see it as the thin of the wedge; you know, one day Sidhartha, the next day hard drugs and all-night parties. My plan was to work on Karen Kapok first and then worry about how I was going to get Ella to come with me. I believe in dealing with one problem at a time.

"Why doesn't your mother like me?" I asked Ella, as we settled on her floor. (Beds, apparently, were for sleeping, not sitting. Mrs. Gerard has a thing about bedspreads as well as insects.)

Ella has a way of just staring at you as though she hasn't heard the question. It means that she's thinking of something diplomatic to say.

"My mother likes you," she mumbled after several seconds. "She thinks you're very—interesting."

But I wasn't going to let Ella slide out of this so easily. I'm like a finely tuned instrument when it comes to reading between the lines—as a great actor should be. I'd heard the pause between "very" and "interesting." Besides, honesty is important in real friendships.

"And I think Hitler was interesting," I retorted. "But that doesn't mean I like him."

Ella laughed. Sometimes I worry that she may grow up to have a laugh like her mother's.

"Stop exaggerating, will you? My mother doesn't think you're anything like Hitler."

"But she doesn't like me," I persisted. I gave Ella a deep, searching look. The kind of look Hamlet was always giving his mother. "I can tell."

Ella made a face. "She likes you fine." Ella made another face. "She just thinks you're a little . . . well . . . you know . . . strange. . . ."

I didn't want to hurt Ella's feelings—after all, she is related to them—so I didn't say that I, personally, think both Mrs. and Mr. Gerard are strange. They're so perfect they might be aliens masquerading in human form.

"And she worries that I don't see as much of my

old friends—you know, since you and I started hanging out."

Ella's "old friends," such as they'd been, were Carla Santini. Carla and Ella—and all Carla's crowd—live in Woodford. Woodford is a "private community." It says so outside the electric security gate. Woodford has mega-expensive houses, rolling lawns, shady streets, and its own leisure center. I'd never even heard of a "private community" before I moved to Deadwood. "Private community" means you aren't supposed to go there unless you live there, are visiting someone by invitation, or are delivering something to someone who lives there, and that there's a guard at the gate to make sure that all riffraff is kept beyond the fortress walls. According to Ella, she and Carla Santini were pretty close in elementary school—when they took dance and music lessons together and went to each other's parties—but that all changed when they hit middle school. It was then that Carla began to blossom and Ella didn't. Carla more or less dumped the quiet and slightly dull Ella and started gathering a more glamorous retinue around her. They were still friendly, of course, as girls whose parents play bridge and tennis and golf together would be, but they weren't exactly twin souls. How could they be? Carla didn't have a soul.

"Pardon me, Ms. Gerard," I said, in a fruity English accent, "but I thought you said that you hardly ever saw Carla. Except for school and rides to school and stuff like that. I thought you said that you've drifted apart."

Ella shrugged. "Yeah, we have. But my mother doesn't know that."

I pursed my lips. "What you're really saying," I said, "is that your mother doesn't like me because I'm not like Carla Santini."

Most of the mothers in Deadwood—and all of the mothers in the private community of Woodford—want their daughters to be like Carla Santini; most of the teachers wish all their students could be like Carla Santini; most of the girls in school wish they could be Carla Santini, even the girls she treats the worst; and as for the boys . . . except for Sam Creek, who seems totally impervious to the Santini charms, any one of them would sell his soul for the chance of getting his tongue into Carla Santini's mouth.

Ella rolled her eyes. "Oh, please . . . will you stop with the Carla Santini obsession for a few minutes?" She pursed her lips, looking at me as if she was wondering how honest she could really risk being. "The thing is . . . ," she went on, slowly and carefully choosing her words.

"The thing is that I'm not your mother's idea of a suitable companion for you." Mrs. Gerard wants Ella to hang out with other well-off, middle-class kids who all go to the same good colleges and eventually have the same narcotic if perfect lives as their parents. She doesn't want her only offspring running around with

22

someone who has the soul and passion of a gypsy and lives in an old house without a microwave.

"Actually," said Ella, her eyes on the thick white carpet, "it's more your mother than you that my mother doesn't think is suitable."

I gazed at her incredulously.

"My *mother*?" Thinking *my* mother isn't suitable is like thinking Santa Claus is a highwayman. My mother is eminently suitable—in an ordinary way. "Not suitable for what?"

Ella squirmed uncomfortably. "It's not big things . . . ," she mumbled, still studying the two-inch pile. "I mean, remember when they met at Parents' Night?"

I nodded my head very slowly. My mother hadn't really said anything about it, just that she'd met the Gerards.

"Yeah?"

Ella squirmed some more. "Well, apparently your mother was wearing filthy old overalls, and she had chopsticks in her hair."

"My mother often has chopsticks in her hair," I answered a little shortly. Because she can never find a hair tie or a barrette. "And if she was in her work clothes, it was because she didn't have time to change."

"You don't have to get defensive with me," said Ella. "I'm just telling you what my mother said."

"But it's ridiculous. What difference does it make what she had in her hair?"

"*I* know it doesn't matter," said Ella. "But my

parents pay attention to stuff like that. They're old-fashioned."

"*Old-fashioned?* Ella, they'd have to be time travelers from the Victorian era to get upset about a pair of chopsticks."

Ella stopped studying the carpet and turned her attention to the CD player. "Forget it," she said. "It isn't important."

"What do you mean, it isn't important?" I threw myself in front of her. "This is the woman who gave me life we're talking about. Whose milk fed my fragile body, whose blood flows through my veins. Of course it's important. What else does your mother have against Karen?"

Ella smiled wryly. "Well, that's one thing."

"What is?"

"That she lets you call her Karen. My mother doesn't like that. She thinks it's disrespectful."

"What else?" I pushed. "There has to be more than that."

Ella sighed. She was no match for me in this kind of thing, and she knew it.

"Well, if you must know, Lola, neither of my parents is too happy about the fact that your mother has three children and no husband."

To her credit, Ella was looking pretty embarrassed.

I was simply stupefied. "What?"

Ella shrugged helplessly.

"I do know this is practically the twenty-first century

and everything, but my folks really are old-fashioned. At least about stuff like that they are. They think single mothers are a threat to society."

Well, you can see their point, can't you? I mean, what hope is there for our culture when a mother lets her sixteen-year-old daughter call her by her first name, wears chopsticks to hold her hair up, and lives without a husband? The barbarians are practically battering down the gates.

I was really interested now. I'd never seen my mother as a social outcast before. It was an idea I could warm to.

"You've got to be joking," I said, even though I knew that she wasn't. "And anyway, single motherhood is a transitory state. I mean, Karen used to be a married mother. It could happen again."

It was Ella's turn to look shocked.

"Your mother was married?" She couldn't have sounded more amazed if she'd just learned my mother used to date the president of the United States.

"Of course she was," I reassured her. "Twice."

"Twice?" Ella frowned. "But I thought you said you were a love child."

I had said I was a love child. I remembered it clearly—now that Ella had reminded me. The truth, that my father, whom I visit at least twice a month, lives in New York and draws pictures of adorable bears and rabbits for a living, is pretty dull. I thought saying I was a love child made me seem more of a tragic, romantic figure. This happens now and then. When you're as creative and imaginative as I am, it can be difficult to keep track of your stories one hundred percent of the time.

"I was a love child," I said, ad-libbing quickly. "I mean, they were madly in love when my mother got pregnant. They weren't planning to get married, of course. My father was a loner by nature, but as soon as they found out that I was on the way, they drove his motorcycle to Las Vegas."

"Las Vegas?" Ella had yet to stop frowning. "I thought your mother always lived in New York. Isn't Las Vegas a little far to go for a wedding?"

You can see why Ella's in all the advanced classes in school. She has a first-rate analytical mind.

"They wanted to honeymoon in New Mexico," I went on, beginning to get into my tale. I could actually see my parents, charging down the highway on a vintage Harley, fueled by love. "New Mexico is a very spiritual place. They wanted to camp in the desert and count the stars." I could see them doing that, too. Their arms were around each other; their heads were sticking out of their tiny tent. It was incredibly romantic.

Ella thought so, too.

"Geez . . . ," she sighed. "My parents went on a cruise to Jamaica for their honeymoon. They stayed on the boat the whole time. They were afraid to go into town."

My voice became heavy and solemn. "Maybe your parents were right to be so cautious," I said very softly.

"New Mexico is where my father met his tragic death."

"Oh, Lola!" Ella's face was the picture of empathetic pain. She has a kind nature, as well as being smart. "I'm so sorry. . . . I had no idea."

I gulped back a tear that even the long years of being fatherless hadn't managed to dry up.

"Of course you didn't." My voice trembled bravely. "He was killed on his way back from town one afternoon." Inspiration flowed through me like current through a wire. "He'd slipped away on the Harley to get my mother her favorite flowers." I stared at the patch of sunlight that illuminated the immaculateness of the carpet. "They found them strewn across the road—" I paused, too choked to continue. But then I forced myself to rally. "They were splattered with blood."

A genuine tear glistened in the corner of Ella's eye.

"Your poor mother . . ." She was practically sobbing. "What a horrible thing for her to go through."

"I know." I shook my head several times very slightly, the way people do when they're remembering something especially painful. "It took her years to get over it. But then she met Elk, the twins' dad. They got married *before* she was pregnant. At least she knew a little domestic bliss. . . ."

I could hear Ella swallow. "What happened to him?"

I hadn't been planning to kill off Elk, too, but the words came tumbling out, beyond my control.

"Elk was a lawyer for Greenpeace," I explained. "He

was on his way to England for a conference." I spent a few more seconds reexamining the patch of light again. "He never came back."

"Oh, no . . ." Ella clutched my hand. "Oh, Lola . . ."

You had to give it to her; she was a terrific audience.

I went on; quietly, in a voice in which time has numbed but not erased the pain.

"His plane went down near Greenland." I could hear the shattering of the plane as it smashed into the ocean. Red and orange flames that burned like the fires of hell exploded in my mind. Men, women, and children screamed without hope. And then, suddenly, a dreadful silence fell over the cold, depthless water. "My mother had to fly out to identify what was left of the body."

Ella's face was whiter than Wonder Bread. "Oh, my God . . ."

I smiled a small but courageous so-it-goes smile. "The twins were only a year old."

Ella shook her head in shock and horror. "Your poor mom, what horrible things she's gone through." She wiped away another tear with the sleeve of her blouse. "I feel like I should apologize to her or something."

Ella was more than capable of apologizing to my mother for having misunderstood her situation. This, however, was not an especially good idea. Elk really is a lawyer for Greenpeace, and he really didn't come back from England—at least not to us—but it wasn't a plane crash that kept him. It was a woman named Margot.

"It's best not to mention the past to her at all," I said quickly. "You know, too many agonizing memories." I sighed as only one who has known real suffering can. "It's ironic, isn't it?" I said. "Your parents think my mother's the destroyer of our social order, and she's merely a victim of Fate."

"I feel so awful." Ella chewed nervously on her lower lip. "I really would like your mother to know that—"

"Whatever happened to the music?" I asked brightly. I picked up the CD Ella had abandoned and put it into the machine.

"Sidhartha!" Ella managed a smile. "I forgot about them!"

"God . . . ," I groaned. "That's like forgetting how to breathe."

I pedaled home beneath a silver crescent of moon, like a nick in the plush velvet of the sky. Ella and I are the only ones who ride our bikes to school. For all I know, we're the only ones who own bikes; most of the kids our age already have cars. But I don't mind. A great actor needs to have good lungs so she can project her voice for the whole theater to hear. Ella stopped taking rides from Carla Santini and her buddies when I convinced her that riding a bike is not only environmentally friendly, but good exercise as well.

I was still aware that Sidhartha existed, but I have

to admit that it wasn't about the greatest band in the history of the world that I was thinking as I rode along. I was thinking about Karen Kapok, my mother.

I couldn't get over the fact that of all the things the Gerards could have held against me—my clothes, my hair, my earrings and nose ring, and my attempts to turn Ella into a vegetarian, to name but a few—they'd chosen Karen Kapok! Ms. Normal. It just shows you how ironic the world really is, doesn't it?

But that, of course, was about to change. I was pretty sure that by the time I got home Mrs. Gerard would already have heard all about my mother's tragic marital history. That meant Mr. Gerard would know by the end of his dinner—assuming, that was, that he made it home for dinner for once. And that meant that by the time the Gerards settled down to watch TV together, their opinion of my mother would have radically altered.

I watched the sliver of moon as I turned up Maple Drive. It hung over the trees like a broken halo.

It was important to me that the Gerards liked me. I wanted them to encourage Ella to see me, not discourage her. Besides, if they didn't like me, I'd never be able to convince them to let Ella go to a Sidhartha concert.

I was whistling as I pulled into our driveway.

Because it was my turn to cook that night (my mother considers herself a potter, not the family chef), I didn't get a chance to phone Ella before supper.

After supper I locked myself in the bathroom for an

hour or so to rehearse my lines for the auditions the next day. This year Mrs. Baggoli had chosen *Pygmalion* for the school's annual production. I knew I was a shoo-in for Eliza—my Cockney accent's a lot better than Audrey Hepburn's in *My Fair Lady*—but I wanted my reading to be perfect. The only competition I had for the lead was, naturally, Carla Santini, if only because no one else would even think of challenging her for a role she wanted. They might try out, but they'd make sure they weren't too good. Carla Santini had starred in everything since she was in kindergarten, and it was tacitly understood that she always got the lead and that everyone else got whatever they got. I'd been too late to try out for the play the year before, but this year I was ready for her. I felt I owed it to all the other mere mortals at Dellwood not to let Carla star this year. Just for a change.

It was almost ten by the time I finally got around to calling Ella. Her father had given her twenty-five bucks for acing her history test, and her mother, who'd just started a new cooking course, had made her own ravioli for supper (Mr. Gerard is always giving Ella money for doing things my mother takes for granted, and Mrs. Gerard is always taking a course in something), but otherwise it was a quiet night.

"I hope you don't mind," said Ella after she'd stopped enthusing about the homemade ravioli, "but I told my folks about your mom."

I pretended to mind—just a little.

"Well . . . ," I said. "I wouldn't want it to get back to my mother that I'd been talking about the tragedies in her life. She's a very private person, you know."

"My parents won't tell anyone," Ella quickly assured me. "They're not gossips."

This is probably true of Mr. Gerard, who doesn't have any time to gossip since he's always working, but it isn't true of Mrs. Gerard. The women of Woodford are a communication system unto themselves. They might not know much about existential theater or postmodern literature, but they know everything that goes on in Dellwood, no matter where it goes on. Gossip is what they do when they're playing golf and shopping and sitting in the sauna together.

"Oh, I know they're not," I said equally quickly. "It's just that it's very personal stuff. . . ."

"My parents were really moved by your mother's story," said Ella. "It made them think."

I smiled at the telephone. "No one's suffering is ever in vain," I softly intoned.

After I hung up, I took a shower, touched up the purple nail polish I was wearing that week to match the lining of my cape, and went to my bedroom to get away from the grunting and shouting of the other members of my family while they played Monopoly in the living room.

When I look back on myself that day, going about my life as if I didn't have a care in the world, it almost makes me weep. How innocent I was! How naive! The poet was right: ignorance is truly bliss. There I was, laughing, talking, working, making spaghetti, eating, going over my script, doing my nails, and brushing my teeth, totally oblivious of the fact that a catastrophe of cosmic proportions was hurtling toward me.

It took me a while to get settled. That's because my bedroom isn't really a bedroom; it's really a sun porch. At least it was until we moved in. My mother, trying to stop the twins from acting so much like twins, decided that each of them should have her own room. So I got the sun porch. (Ordinariness isn't the only thing I have to fight against in my house; gross injustice is another.) Anyway, there isn't any heat in my room, so I had to close all the curtains, plug in the minute and ancient electric heater, and find the chenille bathrobe I got at the Salvation Army so I wouldn't freeze to death. Then I had to go back to the kitchen because I'd run out of candles. Then I had to get my diary out of its secret hiding place where I keep it to safeguard it against the prying eyes of my mother's other children. My father, who is a worrier by nature, is convinced that I'm going to torch the house someday by burning candles, but I prefer candle light to electric. It's so much more atmospheric. Especially when I'm telling the events of the day to my diary. No matter how busy I am, or how exhausted from the slings and arrows of the last twenty-four hours, I write in my diary every single night. My life is extraordinary; I don't want to forget any more of it than I have to.

By the time I was finally in bed with the radio on, my

candles lighted, my diary on my lap, and my pen with the lilac ink in my hand, it was nearly ten forty-five. I started the entry for March the fifth. I had a lot to tell, as always.

I'd had another fight with my mother about my hair at breakfast. My mother thinks that the only suitable hair colors are brown, black, blond, and auburn. She was refusing to let me dye mine blue. She never got over my cutting off all my hair in my Joan of Arc phase, and she still hadn't really come around to the ring in my nose, so she was being especially stubborn this time.

But there were good things, too. My new cape had attracted its share of admiring looks, and Mrs. Baggoli herself had wished me good luck on the auditions the next day. I innocently took these events as good signs.

I'd only gotten as far as everything that had happened in math, my last class of the morning, when the world came to its sudden and horrible end. It wasn't water, and it wasn't ice, and it wasn't even fire. It wasn't even a neutron bomb. It was an announcement.

Wait'll I tell you what happened in the cafeteria today, I was writing.

And then the song that was playing ended, and George Blue, my most favorite DJ in the whole universe, began talking again. I started to listen when I heard the name Sidhartha. I almost wish I hadn't; that the moment had passed right by and left me ignorant but happy for a little longer. I sat there, rigid with horror, the pen dangling from my hand like a withered flower on a severed stalk. I glanced at myself in the mirror next to my bed. If I had to describe the look on my face, I would say it was the expression of a young woman who has lost every reason for living.

"Oh, my God!" I screamed back at the radio. "It can't be! It just can't be! You might as well shoot me now and get it over with!"

"That's right, guys," said George Blue. "You heard it here first. Sidhartha is no more. The boys are going to pursue solo careers."

After I recovered from my initial shock, I raced back outside to call Ella and tell her the earth-stopping news. Ella was devastated. She hadn't been listening to George Blue. She'd been washing her hair. Like Nero fiddling while Rome burned.

"Oh, my God," wailed Ella. "We never even saw them in concert . . ."

The rest of her sentence hung silently in the miles between us: *and now we never will. . . .*

"I don't know how I can face another day," I said softly, trying to hold back the volcano of tears welling inside me. "I just don't know."

My mother was passing on her way back to the living room with a cup of tea. She glanced over at me.

"If you don't get off that phone soon, you won't have to face another day," she informed me.

"Five minutes," I begged. "Just five more minutes."

Ella and I got as far as agreeing to dress in mourning for the rest of the week when my mother came out and did her talking-clock impersonation ("Do you know what *time* it is? It's eleven forty-eight.") and forced me to get off the phone. I went back to my room and put on the new Sidhartha CD. I cried for a while. Then I rubbed off the purple polish and painted my nails jet black. I looked through my music magazines, re-reading every Sidhartha article and interview. I cried some more. I tossed and turned for hours, listening to the wind rip through the trees like monsters clawing out the hearts of babies in their cribs. *Sidhartha is no more!* I silently wailed into the darkness. *Sidhartha is no more!*

I don't know how I ever managed to sleep that night, but I must have dozed, no matter how fitfully, because I knew the instant I was awake: the pain began again.

3

A BRIEF ASIDE

I can't go on with my story until I've explained a little more about Carla Santini. But in order to explain about Carla, I first have to explain about the social structure of Deadwood High. Life is like that, I find. Complicated.

I think of Deadwood High as an ecosystem. It has its groups, and each of them feeds off the others. There are, of course, small grouplettes on the fringe— dope heads, a couple of retro-hippies, a few biker types (but largely without bikes), metal heads, the total untouchables—but basically there are three main groups.

The first group is what I call the BTWs: Born-to-Wins. These are the kids who think of school as a social event. They're popular, attractive, very busy, and usually get an allowance that would support a family of five for a year in Cuba. Their grades may not be the greatest, but they're good enough. The boys are usually all-around athletes and the girls are usually on every committee. Parents and teachers wish these kids would buckle down a little more and treat math and English as though they were as important as the Homecoming

Dance, but otherwise they don't mind them. They know they're not going to be astrophysicists or anything like that, but they also know that they're unlikely to wind up collecting bottles to get the deposit back so they can buy cheap wine.

The second group I call BTRs: Born-to-Run-Everythings. They're the brains and are very goal-oriented. They either dress like the professionals they plan to be, or they're supercool with artistic and intellectual pretensions. They're always seen reading the "right" book or listening to the "right" music. Parents and teachers love these kids.

The BTWs and the BTRs don't interact at all with any of the fringe groups unless it's to torment them, but they're usually civil with each other.

The third group are the Independents. Unlike the kids on the fringe, who are either closet wannabes, or just resigned to the fact that they will never be accepted by any of the "in" groups in this lifetime, the Independents don't care. Because they don't care, they don't get hassled or bullied and are more or less accepted by everyone, if only superficially. Achieving Independent status isn't easy, so there aren't many of them. Maybe eight or ten in the whole of Deadwood High.

I'm an Independent. It's easier for me because I didn't grow up with these kids. Ella should be a BTR—she's at the top of our class, and she lives in the right neighborhood—and she would be if she were a little more like her parents, but Ella was not only very shy and repressed before we met, she's also uncompetitive and unpretentious and finds the BTRs boring. Nobody really paid her that much attention before I moved to Deadwood. She wasn't an Independent; she was just Ella. Now she's an Independent by default because I'm her best friend.

And then, standing alone like a princess on a tower of diamonds, there's Carla Santini.

Carla Santini isn't an Independent. She's a BTW *and* a BTR. She can be anything else she wants to be, but she wouldn't want to be anything else, unless it were God.

Carla Santini is beautiful, rich, intelligent, and revoltingly sophisticated for someone who was born and raised in the depths of New Jersey. She does what she wants; she dresses like a model. If Carla Santini wears something new on Monday, half the girls in the school will be wearing something like it by Friday. And then Carla will never wear hers again. Carla Santini is also one of those people who sees this enormous planet as a single-person dwelling. It baffles me how someone as materialistic, self-centered, and shallow as Carla Santini can be the most popular teenager in Dellwood, but young as I am, I have already learned that there's a lot in this life that doesn't make sense.

After that first conversation in homeroom, Carla Santini didn't come near me for a while. But she watched. I could see her sizing me up as she passed in the hall, tossing her hair and laughing with her friends as though she didn't know I existed. But I made sure that she did. Whether I was in a black phase or a phase of vibrant colors, I stood out: Morticia Addams one day; Carmen the next. And I made sure that I took part in all my classes; especially English. Carla Santini and her brood of admirers monopolized the middle rows in English, forcing everyone else either to the front (where they were always picked on) or to the back (where they fell asleep).

Later that week, I dragged Ella to English early and sat dead center. Ella didn't want to; she always liked to sit to the side at the back, but I pointed out that since there weren't assigned seats we could sit where we wanted. We live in a democracy, don't we? Ella can always be reasoned with. Unlike some of us, she comes from a very reasonable family.

Even Ella admitted that it was worth it, just to see the expression on Carla Santini's face when she strode through the door and saw us sitting in her seats. It only lasted a nanosecond, but it was a beauty: pure, primal rage. Scarlett O'Hara couldn't have done it better. Then, without any hesitation, she screamed out, "I'm bored with sitting in the same place all the time. Let's sit at the back for a change." And she sailed past us, her entourage shuffling after her.

At the end of my first week at Deadwood High, Carla Santini came up to me on the lunch line. She was smiling like a salesman on commission. She has an incredible number of teeth—at least twice as many as the rest of us—each of them perfect and white.

"Hi," she said. "I'm Carla Santini."

As if I didn't know that. It was like Cher coming up to you on the lunch line and saying, "Hi, I'm Cher."

I smiled back. "I know."

Carla's smile became a little less bright but no less toothy. The salesman was about to tell me a price I didn't want to hear. "I know you're new here, Lola," purred Carla Santini, "and you don't understand how things work yet." Her smile solidified. "I've been making allowances for that."

My own smile dimmed slightly. Even though I hadn't heard it, I could tell I wasn't going to like the price.

"So are you going to tell me how things work?" I purred back.

Carla Santini said, "Yes," and stopped smiling. Then she told me. I was sitting in her seat in English. I was attracting too much attention. I was committing social suicide by hanging out with Ella-Never-Had-a-Fella.

"I thought you and Ella were friends." I still had a smile on my face.

"Of course we're friends." She held up her hand, the first and second fingers crossed. "We were like that when we were little. But she doesn't have your potential, does she?" She openly turned and flicked her head to where Ella was sitting with her lunch in front of her, waiting for me. "I mean, look at her. She dresses like a politician's wife. I know she's very sweet, but, let's face it, she's about as exciting as lettuce." The curls shuddered and she looked back to me. "But you . . . you're different. You could really be somebody at Dellwood."

I could hear her adding silently, *If I let you.* That's how Carla Santini works: you don't do anything or get anything unless Carla Santini says so. It's like dealing with the Godfather.

"Wow . . . ," I said. "Then I could die happy."

If it could be bottled, the Santini smile could be used as a chemical weapon.

"It's a lot better than dying *unhappy,*" cooed Carla.

I picked up my tray.

"Thanks for the advice," I said. "Now, if you'll excuse me . . ." I nodded to where Ella was staring at us, her mouth open and a forkful of food hovering in the air beside it, like a politician's wife whose lunch has been disturbed by the arrival of Martians. "My friend is waiting for me."

Those were the first shots fired in what turned out to be a pretty ugly war.

4

I TRY TO LIVE WITH DISASTER

My mother was still sitting at the table, reading the newspaper, when I finally staggered into the kitchen the morning after the end of the world, but the twins had already left for school. Thank the gods for their small mercies. I could face my mother—she, at least, usually tries to act like an adult—but I couldn't have faced her other progeny on that black, black morn. To have to sit with them while they shrieked at each other, babbled about nothing, and spat half-chewed cereal everywhere while my heart was being devoured by the worms of death would have killed me on the spot.

My mother gave me a look when I came in.

"I called you twice," she said, her eyes already back on the article she was reading. "What happened? Did you fall asleep again?"

I took a dragon mug from the shelf, but I was almost too weak to lift it. I leaned against the counter for support.

"I wasn't sleeping," I said in a voice that had lost all trace of joy. Probably forever. "I had a very fraught night." Which was a phenomenal understatement.

My parent responded to this shocking announcement with her usual lack of concern for anyone else, especially me. "I had a very difficult night, too. Someone was playing one of her audio-migraines for hours."

My mother doesn't call what Sidhartha plays "music." My mother calls improvisational jazz "music." Sidhartha's music she calls "audio-migraine."

I poured some coffee into the mug. Very slowly, watching it flow into the cup like blood. "I'm sorry if my music disturbed you." I sighed again. "But I'm afraid it's the only comfort I have right now."

"Well, comfort yourself a little more quietly next time," said my mother.

I picked up my mug and collapsed in the chair across from her.

She finally looked up and noticed that I was all in black, including my lips and eyelids. "So what's it today? You in an *Addams Family* mood, or have you and Ella had a fight?"

I stared into the blackness that filled my cup. "It's nothing," I whispered, the words strained with pain. "You wouldn't understand."

"That's not all you're having for breakfast, is it?" demanded my mother. "You can't go to school on a cup of coffee."

I looked at her as a ghost might look at an old friend who is still alive. "I can't eat anything," I informed her patiently. "It would turn to ashes as it touched my lips."

My mother made a face of exaggerated concentration.

"Bette Davis?" she guessed. "Joan Crawford?" She shook her head. "It can't be Glenn Close."

"This isn't an act," I said hollowly. "This happens to be a day of great unhappiness for me."

"You'll be a lot more than unhappy if you don't at least eat a piece of fruit." She raised her paper. "And you'll wash all that junk off your face before you leave this house, as well. You look like the living dead."

My mother's a potter. Potters aren't like painters or musicians or actors; they're much more pedestrian. It was unusual for her to be so perceptive. This unexpected insight on her part surprised me so much that, even though I must have cried about ten million tears since I heard about the breakup, fresh ones flooded my eyes.

"That's exactly what I am," I sobbed. "I'm the living dead."

"Pretend you're the walking wounded instead," said my mother. "And get yourself something to eat."

"I wonder what really made them break up," Ella was musing as we neared the sprawl of gleaming modern buildings that is Dellwood High. "I mean, 'solo careers' doesn't really tell you much, does it? It's what they always say. It's like when politicians start talking about freedom and liberty; it could mean anything."

"Artistic differences," I decided. "I'm sure I read somewhere that Stu feels stifled by the rest of the group." Stu Wolff was the lead singer and songwriter of Sidhartha, and is, in my humble opinion, one of the greatest geniuses who has ever lived. Maybe even greater than the Bard himself.

"I bet Stu's hard to get along with," said Ella. "You can sort of tell that he's moody."

"Haunted," I corrected her. "All true geniuses are haunted. It's part of what they have to suffer for their art."

"I'm happy I'm so normal," said Ella. "I don't think I could stand the stress of being artistically gifted." She readjusted her book bag on her shoulder and stifled a smile. "Or the pain."

"It isn't easy," I assured her. "It's a great deal to—"

I stopped, paralyzed by the shocking sight in front of my eyes.

"Ye gods!" I wailed. "We really do live in a cultural wasteland. Look at this place, will you? Just look at it!" If my heart weren't already as dead and dry as a bone in the desert, this would have destroyed it for sure.

Ella looked at the rambling brick edifices spread out before us.

"It looks the same as always to me," said Ella.

Ella's the very best friend I've ever had, but if I were being totally honest, I'd have to admit that she doesn't always have much imagination. She's intelligent but not really creative. It comes from growing up with a woman who arranges the spices and canned goods in alphabetical order and has the sheets ironed. That's why she's lucky to have me around. I broaden her horizons. And I benefit from Ella's down-to-earthness, of course. Extremely sensitive and imaginative people need someone steady to balance them.

"That's exactly what I mean!" I strode toward the main building. "One of the most catastrophic events in the history of the universe has just occurred, and everyone here acts as though nothing has happened. You can bet if the president died they'd have the flag at half-mast. And probably have a special assembly where everybody has to observe a moment of silence."

Ella nodded. "Oh, I get what you mean. National mourning."

I steered her into the girls' room so I could put my lipstick and eyeshadow back on.

I flung my makeup bag on the sink. "After all, the death of a president isn't half as devastating as the death of a band like Sidhartha. If the president dies, the vice president takes over for a while, and then they elect a new president. Big deal." I stared at myself in the mirror. The black eyeshadow made me look like a tragic Greek queen who'd just discovered that she married her son or ate her own baby or something like that. "But there'll never be another Sidhartha!" I cried. "It's like the death of the last whale!"

"It's too bad we're not putting on *Moby Dick* this year, isn't it?" said a honeyed voice right behind us. "That would have been perfect for you."

Ella and I looked in the mirror to see one of the stall doors open and Carla Santini waft out. As always, she looked as though at least a dozen photographers were waiting to take her picture, cameras poised. She was wearing DK leggings, a silk Armani top, and spit-polished black boots. Elegant and expensive, but under-stated. Everything about her said, *This is the person you should want to be.*

I smiled my most understated smile. "Only if you played the whale."

Normally I enjoy school. My mother says it's because I like an audience, and what better audience is there than two dozen students and a teacher who can't leave the room for fifty-five minutes?

But that black morning when no birds sang, I couldn't concentrate on anything except the fact that I now lived in a Sidharthaless world.

In history, I stared blindly at Mr. Stiple while he droned on about some war, but all I heard was Stu Wolff singing, "I don't want to hear you say 'never again.' Tell me tomorrow, tell me a lie, but please never tell me 'never again.'"

In math, I gazed raptly at Ms. Pollard while she put equations on the board, but all I saw was Stu Wolff slid-ing across the stage with his guitar on his knee, smiling that endearing, lopsided grin of his.

It was the same in all my other classes. I was so

self-absorbed in gym that I got whacked with a hockey stick and had to sit out most of the period. Ms. Purdue, my gym teacher, said I should try to concentrate on hitting the puck, not being it.

It wasn't until lunch that I began to revive.

Carla Santini and her disciples usually sat anywhere that Ella and I weren't, but that day they sat right behind us.

Because Carla Santini thinks she's Dellwood's answer to Julia Roberts, and because she thinks everybody in the universe is interested in every little thing she does, there is no way you can help overhearing her conversations. Carla will never be a great actor—artistic suffering is as alien to her as wearing perfume is to a swamp rat—but she sure can project.

Ella and I sat in communal silence, thinking about Sidhartha and ignoring Carla, but then something she said caught my attention.

"I had a long talk with Mrs. Baggoli after school yesterday," said Carla. "You know, about *Pygmalion*?"

Pygmalion! I'd been so depressed about Sidhartha that I'd actually let the auditions slip to the back of my mind until then.

There was a gentle murmur of interest from the entourage. Once it had died down, Carla continued. There was nothing in her tone to suggest that modesty was one of her strongest virtues.

"I told her how I thought it was very rigid to stick to the original accents," said Carla. "I mean, we're not

English, and it's not the nineteenth century anymore. . . ."

And Carla Santini couldn't do a Cockney accent to save her life—or even her wardrobe.

"We need to adapt classics to reflect our own times, to make them more immediate and relevant . . ."

"It's hard to relate to characters you can't really understand," agreed Alma. She giggled. "And those clothes . . ."

Tina Cherry, Carla's second-best friend, tittered. "And a flower girl! I mean, really, what's that supposed to be? I mean, she doesn't even work in a florist's, does she?"

Carla squealed with triumph. "That's exactly what I told her. And I pointed out all the successful, meaningful modernizations that have been done in the last twenty years. You know, like *Romeo and Juliet.*"

"Good for you," said Marcia Conroy, the third disciple. "It's about time Mrs. Baggoli woke up and smelled the coffee."

The true significance of what Carla was saying was, of course, not lost on me. I was dumbfounded, truly dumbfounded. Carla Santini, knowing she didn't stand a chance against me when it came to playing an Eliza Doolittle who sold flowers on the streets of London, had decided to change the script. She's incredible, she really is. You almost have to respect her. You certainly have to make sure you never turn your back on her.

"So what'd she say?" asked Tina.

Carla became touchingly coy. I was facing away from

her, but I had no trouble seeing the way she smiled and cocked her head to one side so she'd look shy but mischievous. It's one of her favorite poses. She was undoubtedly tossing her curls as well. It's enough to make you vomit.

"Well, you're not going to believe this, but I told her my idea about changing the location to present-day New York, and making Eliza a checkout girl in a supermarket."

"Uh-huh . . . ," chimed in Alma. "It's a great idea." Alma thinks everything Carla Santini says and does is great. She probably gives Carla a standing ovation when she goes to the bathroom.

"So what'd she say?" pressed Tina, whining slightly with impatience.

"Yeah," said Marcia, "tell us what she said."

"Well . . ." Carla paused dramatically. The suspense was really killing them. "Mrs. Baggoli said she thought it was a really excellent idea." The table behind us erupted in girlish squeals of delight. "She said she'd been thinking it was time to do something a little different," Carla went on, nobly controlling her own excitement but not quite keeping the smug triumph out of her voice, "and she thought my idea was just the thing."

"That's incredible!" gushed Alma. "That's truly incredible!"

Tina and Marcia, like myself, were at a loss for words. All they managed were a few awestruck "Gee"s.

Carla's laughter rumbled around us. "Didn't I tell you you wouldn't believe it?"

Carla was right, I didn't believe it. The major problem with Carla Santini—aside from her character, her personality, and her annoying personal habits—is that she was born and raised in Deadwood. As were all her friends. She established her image and territory in kindergarten. She can make anybody believe anything. Even teachers are fooled by Carla. Even Ella had been fooled. But Mrs. Baggoli? Mrs. Baggoli has done repertory all over the country; she once directed an off-Broadway play; she even had some small parts in a couple of movies; *and* she's traveled just about all over the world. I couldn't believe that someone of Mrs. Baggoli's sophistication and worldliness could possibly be fooled by Carla.

"Carla Santini strikes again!" crowed Alma.

Out of the mouths of yes-girls . . .

"I really have to hand it to you, Carla," said Marcia admiringly. "You always go after what you want, don't you?"

"And she always gets it," I whispered to Ella.

Carla laughed with what passed in her for good nature. It sounded like a knife going through live tissue.

"My parents didn't raise any losers," said Carla.

Ella gave me a look. I could tell from the way her mouth was turned down that Ella thought that my parents had.

5

THE SHOW MUST GO ON

Perhaps it was that look of futility and hopelessness on the face of the best friend I have ever had; perhaps it was the knowledge that—even if they didn't know it—the rest of the student body was depending on me to strike the first blow for freedom from the tyranny of Carla Santini; perhaps it was the sense of outrage I felt over Carla Santini's backstage maneuverings; perhaps it was a combination of these things, but even though my grief still flowed through me like ice water, I forced myself to rally in the afternoon. I was now more determined than ever. The only way Carla Santini was going to get that part was if she killed me.

I was a little late for the auditions because I had to go to the girls' room after English to touch up my makeup. Mrs. Baggoli broke off when I burst through the door of the auditorium.

"You're just in time, Lola," boomed Mrs. Baggoli. "I was telling the others about the idea I've had for our production of *Pygmalion*."

"The others" were my fellow drama club members, all of whom were clutching their scripts and watching me walk down the middle aisle. All, that was, except Carla Santini. As amazing as it was for her to play costar, Carla was gazing raptly at Mrs. Baggoli as though Mrs. Baggoli were God and she were Moses.

Relief swept through me with such force that I almost felt weak. It was Mrs. Baggoli's idea we were going with, not Carla Santini's. I knew Mrs. Baggoli couldn't be fooled!

Before I had a chance to ask Mrs. Baggoli what her idea was, she told us.

Mrs. Baggoli had decided to set *Pygmalion* in modern-day New York. Henry Higgins would be a professor at N.Y.U. and Eliza Doolittle would be a checkout girl in a supermarket. The revised scripts would be ready by the end of the week. For now, we'd just wing it.

I felt like I'd fallen down the rabbit hole with Alice. I glanced around at my fellow thespians. They were all looking serious and nodding their heads.

Carla Santini went off like the fountain at Lincoln Center.

"What a brilliant idea!" she shouted. "This will give the play a new resonance, an immediacy for today!"

"And it also means we won't have to put on those stupid accents," muttered one of the boys.

I gaped in horror at my favorite teacher. "You mean it's *your* idea?"

"Yes, Lola," said Mrs. Baggoli. She gave me an amused look. "I know I'm just a high-school teacher, but I am capable of thought."

There was a ripple of laughter.

I laughed along with my usual good humor. "Oh, I know that," I said quickly. I turned up the wattage on my smile. "It's just that Carla said at lunch that it was *her* idea—that's all. That's why I was surprised."

Mrs. Baggoli looked from me to Carla. "Oh, really?"

Carla gazed back at her with the innocence of an angel. "I don't know what she's talking about, Mrs. Baggoli." She shrugged, an angel trying to understand the workings of the treacherous human mind. "She must have been eavesdropping when I was telling my friends about your idea at lunch and misunderstood...." Her words trailed off meaningfully. *And gotten it wrong as usual.*

I was about to explain that I hadn't gotten the wrong idea, that Carla presented Mrs. Baggoli's idea as her own, but Mrs. Baggoli didn't give me a chance.

"Let's start with Colonel Pickering, shall we?" she asked, and she picked up her script and sat down.

Because the drama club is small, everyone tries out for a major role. After she decides who's gotten the leads, Mrs. Baggoli assigns the minor parts. Anyone who's left over gets to be stage manager, or understudy for the entire play, or something like that.

After Colonel Pickering, we went to Henry Higgins. And then we got to Eliza herself.

Susan Leder and Janeann Simmons went first, with all the passion and enthusiasm of soldiers crawling out of a foxhole to certain death by enemy fire.

At last, I took my place on the stage. I didn't really need the script because I already knew most of the part by heart, but I held it in front of me anyway. For effect.

"I'm ready whenever you are," called Mrs. Baggoli. "Begin with 'You got no right to touch me.'"

I glanced at my script. What Eliza actually says (whimpering) is, "Nah-ow. You got no right to touch me." I took a deep breath. I looked straight at Mrs. Baggoli.

"Nah-ow," I said in an accent that would have made Henry Higgins jump for joy. "You got no right to touch me."

You could hear everyone making an effort not to laugh.

Except Mrs. Baggoli and Carla Santini.

"No, Lola," said Mrs. Baggoli between hearty chuckles. "It's set in New York now, remember? You can drop the Cockney. Try it again."

I nodded like the true professional I am. I repeated the line in my head. I took another deep breath.

"Nah," I said. "Ya got no right t' touch me."

This time everyone laughed; though no one louder than Carla Santini, of course.

"Lola," gasped Mrs. Baggoli. "You're not trying out for *Serpico*. Let's do it again."

I walked over to the edge of the stage. "But Mrs. Baggoli, I don't know what this girl is like anymore. I knew who she was when she was an English flower seller, but I don't have a clue now."

Mrs. Baggoli's smile thinned slightly. "I thought this was going to make it easier, not harder," she announced.

"Yeah, I know." I shook my head. "But the thing is, I have to know something about this girl." How could I do Eliza's accent if I didn't know anything about her? It was like painting the portrait of someone you'd never seen. "Is she Italian? Irish? Black? Puerto Rican? Vietnamese? Thai? Serbian? Czech? Russian?" All Mrs. Baggoli had to do was ask and she would have had it. After all, I'd lived in New York all my life—excepting my nearly one year in the wasteland of Deadwood—so there wasn't an accent ever heard in the grand canyons of the metropolis that I couldn't imitate.

"What about Polish?" shouted Bryan Perkowski. "What do you have against us?"

"Never mind the Poles," said Beth Millstein. "What about the Jews? You have something against the Jews?"

"You know," chipped in Carla, "she could be Korean. There are lots of Koreans in New York, aren't there, Lola?"

Mrs. Baggoli clapped loudly. "Let's all settle down, shall we?" She smiled at me. "Her name's Doolittle, Lola," said Mrs. Baggoli. "She's just a poor white girl who was born in New York. Use your own accent."

Nodding, I went back to my place on the stage. I closed my eyes, imagining myself in a red jacket with a nametag pinned to the pocket: Hi! My Name's Liz. I heard the Muzak and the rumble of shoppers' conversations; I heard someone drop a bottle of oil on aisle three; I heard kids whining and the baggers fooling around; I heard people grumbling about the prices and the state of the tomatoes. I ran a soup can over the scanner. My fingers touched the keys of the register. I thought about my father, Mr. Doolittle. My father was a garbage man and a hopeless drunk. My mother died when I was little, probably from drugs. I left home when I was sixteen. I shared a grungy apartment with two other checkout girls who also came from dysfunctional families. There was a boy I liked who worked on one of the delivery trucks. He had three tattoos and a gold nose ring. I could see this boy clearly. His name was— I opened my eyes. I had no idea what his name was. It could be Tom, or Tony, or Jesus, or Vinny, or Joseph, or Onion, for all I knew.

"We'd all appreciate it if you could do this this afternoon," boomed Mrs. Baggoli. "There are other people waiting to audition, you know."

"I'm sorry," I apologized. "I really am."

I took a deep breath.

It was Liz Doolittle from Brooklyn who spoke next. But girls from Brooklyn don't whimper, no matter what the stage directions say.

"F— off, turkey," snarled Liz Doolittle. "Keep your f—in' hands off me."

Everybody cracked up at that. I was afraid Mrs. Baggoli was going to choke to death, she was laughing so hard.

"I don't think the PTA's going to think very much of that," she said when she was finally capable of speech. "But I can see that I may need your help polishing the modernization."

Carla Santini gave me one of her full-dental smiles. I had no trouble interpreting its meaning: *It'll give you something to do—now that you won't be Eliza.*

Mrs. Baggoli didn't let outsiders sit in on the auditions, so Ella waited in the library until I was done.

She started shutting her books as soon as I came through the door.

"Well?" Ella demanded in a loud whisper. "How'd it go?"

I flung my cape over my shoulder. "I'm pleased to be able to announce that after a rocky start our heroine gave a brilliant reading."

I really was pleased with what I'd done in the end. I was sure that when the parts were posted the next morning my name would be the one next to Eliza Doolittle. I explained about the rocky start as we left the library.

"Oh God . . . ," groaned Ella. "What a nightmare."

"It happens," I said philosophically. Wasn't it Shakespeare who said that you can't be wise if you've never been a fool? "There isn't a great actor in the history of the theater who hasn't done something even worse. I read that Robert De Niro once got up on a stage and started performing the wrong play."

"Really?" Ella grinned wickedly. "Wouldn't it be great if that happened to Carla Santini?"

Mentioning Carla Santini's name was like mentioning Satan's. She instantly appeared, walking across the parking lot with Mrs. Baggoli. Carla drives a red BMW convertible. Mrs. Baggoli drives an old black Ford.

"Speak of the devil," said Ella. She gave me a look. "So how did Carla do?"

"She was good." If you're going to be a great actor, you have to learn to be magnanimous. I winked. "But she wasn't as good as I was."

"You can't tell from looking at her, though, can you?" said Ella.

I followed her gaze. Carla and Mrs. Baggoli had stopped by Mrs. Baggoli's car. Mrs. Baggoli was nodding as she climbed into the driver's seat. Carla was animated about whatever it was she was going on about. Her curls were bouncing all over the place. She didn't look like someone who knew she'd just lost her chance to play Eliza.

I whipped my cape over my shoulder and bent to unlock my bike.

"She probably thinks that if she talks long enough, Mrs. Baggoli will give her the part just to make her shut up."

6

THINGS GET BOTH BETTER AND EVEN WORSE

Even though my soul was withering like a rose deprived of sunlight and water, I was in a pretty good mood Tuesday night.

As I'd told Ella, although I'd admittedly gotten off to a less than spectacular start with my reading, I was confident that I'd performed significantly better than Carla in the end. I mean, I'd have to had, wouldn't I? Expecting Carla to identify with a poor supermarket checkout girl was like expecting the Queen of England to identify with a mud wrestler from Alabama.

And although playing Eliza wasn't the same as knowing that Sidhartha was out there—a spiritual satellite in the great nothingness of the universe—it did give me something positive to do with my grief. I would use it to be the best Eliza Doolittle I could be, no matter what her ethnic background. It's what all great actors do, of course: they put aside the disappointments and tragedies of their own lives and throw themselves into their work. The show, as they say, must always go on.

Self-doubt didn't kick in until sometime between

Tuesday night when I fell asleep to the Stu Wolff classic, "Everything Hurts," and Wednesday morning when I woke up with a heart as cold and as heavy as Mount Everest.

I dreamed about Carla Santini. She was up on the stage of a packed auditorium. The spotlights were on her, and her arms were filled with dozens of orchids. I was standing in the wings. I was wrapped in my cape because the costume I should have been wearing was on Carla Santini. Just as the flowers that were meant for me were in her arms, and the applause that should have been mine was falling on her ears. I was crying very, very softly. As the audience erupted in shouts of "Bravo! Bravo!" Carla turned to face me. She smiled at me the way she had during my audition.

My eyes opened to the stain that looks like an amoeba on the ceiling over my bed. From one cell all life grew. One day there's just this microscopic dot floating around in some swamp, and a few billion years later, I'm lying in bed wondering how I could be so stupid.

How *could* I be so stupid? Why had I been so certain I was going to get the lead? Had I forgotten how Mrs. Baggoli had laughed at me? Had I forgotten what she had said? *You're not trying out for* Serpico. . . . *I don't think the PTA's going to think very much of that. . . . We'd all appreciate it if you could do this this afternoon. . . . I thought this was going to make it easier, not harder. . . . I can see that I'm going to need your help polishing the modernization. . . .*

All she'd said to anyone else was "Thank you," or "Try it again," or "Could you speak up a little?" At no one else had she rolled her eyes and sighed.

I'd gone too far. This is something my parents often wrongly accuse me of doing, but this time I really had. I'd figured Mrs. Baggoli would be impressed by my desire to know the character I was portraying in every intimate detail and to make her real, but now that I thought about it, she'd been more annoyed than impressed. What convinced me of that wasn't the expression I could remember on Mrs. Baggoli's face, but the look I could remember on Carla Santini's. That smile . . . it was the smile of Iago as he watched Othello storm off to ruin his life.

I jumped out of bed and dressed in record time. I raced into the kitchen, grabbed something for lunch, and was out of the house before my mother could yell at me for not having any breakfast. I had to get to school before everyone else. If I really wasn't going to play Eliza, I wanted to be the first to know. And I wanted to be alone when I found out. I could handle it—after all, rejection is part of the creative process; as painful as it is necessary for true growth and greatness—but I'd need a little time to prepare myself, to decide how I was going to play my defeat.

It wasn't something I'd thought about before. I had a pretty good idea how Carla Santini would play it if she got the losing role. When she stole Anya Klarke's boyfriend last spring, Carla had managed to act as though *she* and not Anya were the injured party. It was Anya who was generally treated as though she were an evil witch and Carla who sat around polishing her halo. There was no way I was going to let that happen to me.

By the time the green fields of Dellwood High finally came into view, I was sweating and breathless, and my mascara was running. There were a few cars in the parking lot, including Mrs. Baggoli's old Ford. That meant she'd posted the results. I jumped the curb in front of the main building and rode straight to the entrance of the auditorium.

Carla, Alma, Tina, and Marcia were standing in front of the doors, theirs heads together as though conjuring a spell. If I'd been quicker, or if I ever bothered to oil my bike, I might have gotten away before they saw me. But I wasn't, and I didn't. My brakes screeched as I tried to slow down enough to retreat.

Like cows, they turned together. There was no sweat on Carla or her friends. They all looked as though they were waiting for the photographer. Considering the amount of makeup they all wore, they must have been up at dawn.

"Well, will you look what the wind's blown in," cooed Carla.

I knew that coo. If it had been a weapon, it would have been a submachine gun. Carla was happy. I hadn't gotten the part.

But a great actor acts, whether she got the part or not.

I smiled. "I couldn't stand the suspense," I said, as if I were interested but personally unconcerned. "I had to see how the casting went."

"Oh, did you?" Carla smiled. A switchblade joined the Santini arsenal.

"Yeah." I forced myself to smile back. A great actor puts the play before her own petty needs and desires. She doesn't sulk or get grumpy when she loses out to a lesser talent. She is generous even in the most ignominious defeat. "Well," I said brightly, "are congratulations in order?"

Alma, Tina, and Marcia all looked to Carla. Carla just stared at me.

When no one responded I went on. "I can't wait to see what part I got. No matter what, it's going to be a great production."

"If it is a great production, it'll be thanks to Carla," said Alma. I thought she meant because Carla was going to play Eliza, but she didn't. "I mean, whose idea was it to update the play in the first place?"

Surprise, I've noticed, can often provoke honesty.

"Well, actually, it was—"

Carla cut me off before I could say "Mrs. Baggoli's."

"Oh please . . . ," she sneered. The faculty of Dellwood High would have been pretty shocked to hear the venom in her lovely, well-modulated voice. "Stop pretending, will you? You'd rather kill yourself than play anyone but Eliza, and you know it."

I was about to say that, actually, I'd rather kill her, but

before I could even open my mouth Carla stepped right up to me, as though she were going to invite me behind the school to have a fight.

"Well, you're going to wish you had killed yourself when I get through with you," she whispered.

Alma, Tina, and Marcia smiled, nodding.

I felt like Macbeth, but with one extra witch.

I flung my cape over my shoulder, defiantly. Carla jumped back with a cry of surprise.

"Are you threatening me?" I asked in a calm and reasonable voice.

Carla gave me one of her "What's this bug doing on my sleeve?" looks.

"You've gone too far," said Carla Santini in this dead-calm voice. "You always have to have things your way, but this time you've really gone too far." She smiled. It wasn't what you could call a pleasant sight. "I didn't think you were this stupid," she continued. "But now it's time you learned your place."

And with that she swept away, the other three hurrying behind her.

I knew, of course, why Carla was so furious, but I pushed my bike up to the list on the door anyway. I had to see it for myself. I started at the top of the list and worked my way down. Henry Higgins: Jon Spucher. Colonel Pickering: Andy Lightman. Mrs. Higgins: Carla Santini. Eliza Doolittle: Lola Cep.

* * *

Carla Santini is not the sort of person to slink quietly away into a corner after a defeat. There are a lot of negative things you can say about Carla, but giving up easily isn't one of them.

That's why Ella and I wound up sitting near Carla at lunch. When we got to the cafeteria, Carla and her friends were already at our table, talking and laughing as though she were a total stranger to jealousy and anger.

"There're a couple of spaces in the far corner," said Ella, starting to veer to the right.

I grabbed her wrist. "We'll sit where we always sit."

She gave me one of her looks. "What?" hissed Ella. "You want to sit in Carla's lap?"

It was true. In order to sit where we always sat I'd be in Carla's lap, and Ella would be in Tina's.

"Okay, Okay," I said, "not exactly where we always sit. There're two empty chairs behind their table. We'll sit there."

"Why can't you ever just lie low?" muttered Ella, but she muttered as she followed me across the room.

Surprise surprise, Carla Santini was talking about the play.

Enthusiastically.

"Actually," she was saying as we took our seats, "the character of Mrs. Higgins is more interesting than Eliza's in many ways. I've always thought of her as a symbol of feminism."

Ella glanced at me as she began to remove a series of

pastel plastic containers from her lunch bag. Mrs. Gerard's cooking class had moved on to salads.

"Even though she's not the female lead, it's a part with depth and true contemporary resonance."

I was happy I hadn't started eating yet; I might have been sick.

Carla sighed. It was a sigh full of sadness and regret.

"To be totally honest," said Carla, "I think Mrs. Baggoli made the right decision."

There were a few gasped protests and a couple of sympathetic snorts.

"Really," insisted Carla. "I mean, what is Eliza when you get down to it? She's a loser, isn't she? She's illiterate, she's ignorant, she's in a dead-end job with no future or opportunities. . . ." She sighed again. Poor Eliza. "She'll probably end up on drugs or as a prostitute—what else is there for her?"

I could feel her shudder delicately but distastefully behind me. I felt a few Santini curls hit my head.

"Now that I think about it, I really don't think I could identify with someone like that," said Carla. She laughed sharply. "It takes a thief to catch a thief, doesn't it?"

"Huh?" said Alma.

A few more curls slapped against me. Carla was rolling her eyes.

"You *know*," moaned Carla, "it takes a thief to know how a thief thinks. . . ." You could almost hear her start to purr. "Just as it takes a low-life to know how a low-life feels."

Alma, Tina, and Marcia all collapsed in hysterics.

I could have turned around and said something. You know, something subtle but apt. Like, "Well then, it is amazing that you didn't get the part, isn't it?" But I didn't. To answer would be to play right into Carla's game. To ignore her and act as though I hadn't heard what she said would drive her nuts.

I raised my juice container over the table. "Let's toast," I said loudly to Ella. "After all, this is really a celebratory lunch, isn't it?"

Ella's expression was about as celebratory as a death mask, but she nodded and held up her stainless-steel thermos.

"To *Pygmalion!*" I cried gaily.

"To *Pygmalion,*" muttered Ella. And immediately afterward and much louder she said, "So, what do you think of all the rumors?"

Despite the initial disinterest of the Deadwood High School populace toward the death of a legend, there were now more rumors about Sidhartha going around than Carla Santini had teeth.

The reason the band split up was because Bryan Jeffries, the drummer, was a drug addict.

No, it was because Jon Waldaski, the bass player, was dying of AIDS.

Because Steve Maya, the lead guitarist, was an alcoholic.

Because Stu Wolff was an alcoholic and/or a drug addict.

Because Stu wanted to change his image.

Because Stu and Steve did nothing but fight—because Stu stole Steve's girlfriend.

Because Stu and Steve did nothing but fight—because Stu wouldn't let Steve play his songs in the band.

Because Bryan attacked Jon with a snare drum.

Because Stu broke Bryan's jaw.

Because Jon was suing the others for not giving him credit for songs that were his.

Blahblahblah . . .

"I can't believe Bryan's into drugs," I said. "Stu wouldn't tolerate it. He has too much integrity." It went without saying that, despite the historical connection between genius and mind-altering substances, we had dismissed the accusations of drug addiction against Stu automatically. Not only did he have integrity, he was passionate about his music. There was no way he would risk it for some superficial thrill.

Ella started arranging the plastic containers in an orderly line. She's not related to Marilyn Gerard for nothing. "Maybe he didn't know at first," said Ella. "Maybe he only just found out."

I opened my beat-up Zorro lunch box. I bought it in a junk store on the Lower East Side. I've always loved Zorro. I guess it's the cape.

"He's too smart." I took out the chunk of cheese and the apple I'd packed before I raced from the house. "He'd have noticed right away."

"Well, maybe they have creative differences," said Ella, opening each container in turn.

I wiped the clay from my apple. Everything in our house is covered with clay. It's what you call an occupational hazard. "I think it's more likely to be personality clashes. From what I've read, Steve can be really selfish and bossy."

It was at that point that Carla Santini more or less joined our conversation.

"Did I tell you?" she shouted. "My father just called me on my cell phone to tell me what he found out about Sidhartha."

Carla's father is a phenomenally successful media lawyer who knows everybody who'd been famous for even fifteen seconds. He dines with movie stars. He gets drunk with famous musicians. He golfs with producers, directors, and television personalities. When she was six, Marlon Brando took Carla Santini on his knee and kissed the top of her head. She has a photo to prove it.

"You're kidding!" shrieked Alma. "You mean your dad *talked* to *Stu*?" She sounded as if she were reading her lines from a cue card.

The air itself quivered with the nodding of Carla's head.

"Stu told my father that he's really angry about all the rumors that have been circulating about them," blared Carla. "He hates the way the press always misrepresents things."

The disciples all murmured sympathetically—as though they cared what the press did.

"So guess what they're going to do?" squealed Carla, loudly enough to get a response from the house across the street. She paused dramatically.

My curiosity was greater than my disdain for anything Carla Santini might have to say. I leaned back in my seat just a tiny bit. Was she going to say that Sidhartha wasn't disbanding after all?

When not even Alma hazarded a guess, Carla took a deep, meaningful breath. "They're going to have a big farewell concert at Madison Square Garden to say good-bye to all their friends and fans." If anyone else in the universe had made that announcement, she would have sounded excited; Carla sounded as though it had been her idea.

Alma, Tina, and Marcia all started to sigh and screech, but Carla wasn't finished yet.

"And guess what else?" she demanded.

I swear to God that the three of them gasped, "What?"

"My father already has seats in the press box."

Alma, Tina, and Marcia all went off like smoke alarms, but I didn't blink. So this was Carla's revenge. She didn't even like Sidhartha that much. She just wanted to get even with me.

"But that's not the best part," said Carla once the noise had died down. "There's going to be an awesome party afterward for all their closest friends." If I'd had a pair of scissors on me, I think I would have turned around and cut off her hair. "And guess who already has an invitation?"

I don't know why I did it. I really and truly don't. It wasn't like I planned it or anything. But the smug triumph in Carla Santini's voice really annoyed me.

I turned my head so that I was officially part of the conversation.

"It just so happens that Ella and I do," I said sweetly.

Carla Santini's eyes locked with mine.

"Oh, really?" Smug triumph now had a companion: sarcasm. Carla didn't believe me. Which meant that no one else did either.

I, however, was cool and unruffled; I was self-possessed. Ignoring the horrified expression on Ella's face, I met Carla's eyes.

"Yeah," I said. "Really."

There were a few darting glances and smirks around the table. Carla caught them all. A smile slipped over her face like a snake through water.

"And just how did *you* manage that?" she asked.

"The same way you did," I immediately answered. "Through parental connections."

"*Connections?*" Carla made a sound that would have been a snort if a pig and not a perfect person were making it. "What connections do *you* have, except to the phone?"

To be a truly great thespian you have to be able to do more than act from a script. You have to be able to improvise. I improvised.

"My mother got them. Marsh Foreman bought a piece from her in the summer. I met him when he came to pick it up. He remembered that I liked Sidhartha, so he gave my mother two invitations."

This wasn't technically true, of course, but it was definitely possible. Marsh Foreman was Sidhartha's manager. It stood to reason that he had money to spend on handcrafted goods. Lots of rich people bought my mother's stuff. Why shouldn't Marsh Foreman be one of them?

Carla arched one eyebrow. "Your mother must be some potter."

"Yeah," I agreed. "She is." Then I laughed as if suddenly understanding something—something too silly for words. "Oh, you think she makes bowls and plates and stuff like that. . . ." Bowls and plates and stuff like that are what my mother does make, but there are lots of other potters who aren't obsessed with use and function. "Oh, no, my mother makes things like six-foot fish in suits. In fact, the piece that Marsh Foreman bought was a badger, a racoon, and a fox playing Monopoly." I smiled. "He put it in his garden."

7

ME AND MY BIG MOUTH

Carla's announcement lifted my soul to the heavens themselves. All was not lost, after all. Sidhartha was giving one last concert! Ella and I hadn't missed the chance of seeing them; we now had the chance to see them at their very very best in a concert that would be part of the rock legend for centuries to come. Decades from now, Ella and I would be telling our grandchildren how we were at Sidhartha's farewell gig—how we'd even gone to the party afterward and met Stu Wolff.

Ella, however, had a slightly different take on things.

"I really can't believe you sometimes, Lola," said Ella. She dumped a bag of chips into a shining dark blue bowl. No clay dust or outrageous colors here. Mrs. Gerard was at her cooking class, or pushing a book trolley around the hospital, or something like that, so Ella was fixing our snack for a change. "I really can't. What exactly do you think is wrong with you?"

"You're over-reacting," I said with my usual reasonable calm. I helped myself to a chip. "I'm sure you would have said the exact same thing if you'd been me."

Hand-reared by Marilyn Gerard, colonel in the war

against dirt and disorder, Ella automatically brushed my crumbs from the counter.

"If I were you I wouldn't know any better, would I?" she asked. "I'd be crazy enough to tell Carla Santini that Marsh Foreman had invited me to the Sidhartha goodbye party."

I flashed her one of my peppiest smiles.

"Be fair," I begged. "I told her you were invited, too."

Ella gave me a long, hard look. She sighed. "Have you really gone insane?" she asked quietly. "What were you thinking? Doesn't your brain ever get in touch with your mouth?"

"I was thinking what a pain in the neck Carla is— that's what I was thinking," I replied honestly. "It drives me nuts the way she's always tossing her hair around and smiling. She acts like she's visiting royalty and the rest of us are just a bunch of lepers."

Ella put the juice on the counter. "Okay, so Carla Santini has insurmountable ego problems. That's beside the point."

I slapped the gleaming marble counter with my hand. "I disagree. That's exactly the point, in my humble opinion. If Princess Carla didn't start practically every sentence she utters with 'I this' or 'My that' I would never have opened my mouth."

And maybe if Carla had bothered to congratulate me on being Eliza instead of threatening my life.

Ella sidestepped my irrefutable argument.

"But you did open your mouth," said Ella. "I tried to

tell you that if Carla says she's going to put you in your place, she means it. And what do you do? You open your enormous mouth, that's what you do." She shook with frustration. "You handed her exactly what she needs to humiliate and ridicule you for the rest of your life." She scowled. "And me, too, probably."

Ruminating, I bit into another chip. "I don't know about that," I said slowly. "I mean, it depends, doesn't it?"

Ella handed me a glass. "Depends on what? Whether or not someone drops a gold record on her head at the party and she develops amnesia?"

I stared at the glass for a minute. I was used to finger-prints on my glasses. This one sparkled the way they do in dishwasher detergent advertisements.

"Well . . . ," I said at last. "It kind of depends on whether we go or not, doesn't it?"

Ella spilled grape juice all over the counter.

"On whether we go or not?" she shrieked. She was so upset that she wasn't even mopping up the juice. She was just standing there, staring at me in stupefied horror. "What do you mean? We're not going to the Sidhartha party, Lola. This may have slipped your mind, but we haven't exactly been invited."

I waved this objection aside. "You don't have to be invited to a party like that," I assured her. "You just crash. There are people in New York who never go out unless it's to crash some celebrity bash."

"Well, I'm not from New York," said Ella between

clenched teeth. "And anyway, my mother would never let me go to party like that, even if it were being held next door, and you know it. Not without her. Are you planning to take my mother with us?"

What a thought! Mrs. Gerard stopped listening to music when the Beatles broke up. And although I'm pretty sure that she must have had a youth, I'm also pretty sure that it hadn't been what you'd call wild unless you were comparing it with the life of a drop of paint. I'd rather have taken the Pope on my honeymoon than taken Mrs. Gerard to the Sidhartha party.

"We can work around your mother," I informed Ella. "She doesn't have to know."

"Are you kidding?" Ella's voice was unnervingly shrill. "There's no way on earth you and I are going to sneak into the city for a concert without my mother finding out. Never mind going to a party afterward. My mother wants to know where I am every minute of the day and night."

Unfortunately, there was a certain amount of truth in this. Mrs. Gerard does everything but make Ella punch in and out on a time clock. It isn't that she doesn't trust her—Ella is an incredibly trustworthy teenager if you ask me—it's that she worries about her all the time. If Ella's ten minutes late getting home, her mother will be at the door before she turns in the front path. My mother might worry about me if she knew I was out on a motorcycle with someone for whom speed limits are merely suggestions, but otherwise she's too busy worrying about a trillion other things to time my comings and goings. This, however, was not the moment to start agreeing with Ella.

"How do you know she'd find out?" I demanded. "There must be at least a dozen ways we could manage to go into The City and stay out the entire night without her ever finding out. All we have to do is figure out what they are."

Ella gaped. "Tell me the truth, Lola. Are you on drugs?"

I laughed. A person could never get away with taking drugs in my house. My mother can just look at me and know if I'm about to get my period or not.

I scattered some more crumbs around. "I will be if I don't get to that concert."

Ella stared at the puddle of juice on the counter with sightless eyes. "Maybe you should just let Carla have this," she said. "You know . . . you got the lead. Let her have the party and everything."

Let her have the party and everything? I could hardly believe my ears. How could Ella suggest that we just give up like that? Carla Santini may think that she's God, but that doesn't make me Jesus. "You're the one who's on drugs," I retaliated. "A few minutes ago you said I'd already given her the weapon she needed to humiliate and ridicule us for the rest of our lives, and now you want me to load her weapon and pull the trigger."

Ella turned her attention from the spreading purple

stain to me. "But that's exactly what you are doing. If you'd kept quiet and let her lord the concert over us for a few years, she'd have been happy. Now she's not going to rest till the whole school knows that we don't really have invitations."

"Exactly!" I was practically shrieking with emotion. "That's why we *have* to go." I held my head high. "It's a matter of pride."

Ella sighed with exasperation. "Pride goeth before a fall," she muttered.

"Nothing ventured, nothing gained," said I. I picked up another chip. "I refuse to give in. There's no way I'm handing Carla a consolation prize."

"It wouldn't be a consolation prize." Ella's eyes were back on the juice. "It'd be more like . . . like a . . ."

I leaned closer to her. "Like a what?"

Ella shrugged. "Like an offering to unfriendly spirits so they leave you alone."

"*Doodeedoodeedoodeedoodee* . . . What is this?" I joked. "*The Twilight Zone?*"

Ella looked at me, but she wasn't smiling.

"You don't know Carla the way I do," said Ella in total seriousness. "You weren't here when she was after Kali Simpson."

"Who's Kali Simpson?"

Ella shrugged again. "She was just this girl who used to go to Dellwood. But she and Carla had a fight about something and Carla decided to destroy her."

"You're making me tremble." I trembled.

80

"You wouldn't be so flippant if you'd seen the way she treated Kali," said Ella. "She stopped talking to her and everyone else stopped, too. Anytime Kali was around she'd start badmouthing her, and the disciples would all laugh. She made up all these lies and spread them around the school—you know, that Kali was shoplifting . . . that Kali was having sex with half the boys in school . . . that her mother was an alcoholic . . ." It was Ella's turn to tremble, but she wasn't acting. "It was really horrible. The only person who really stuck by Kali was Sam Creek, and even he couldn't help her in the end."

Sam Creek, Deadwood's token bad boy, is also its other great Independent. With his black leather jacket, his Celtic tattoo, his beaded dreads, his multitude of piercings, and his attitude, Sam Creek is the antithesis of Carla Santini. He's also the only guy who doesn't worship her.

"So what happened?" I asked. "Did Carla turn Kali into a frog?"

Ella gave me a "don't start" look.

"The Simpsons moved, that's what happened." Ella stared into my eyes. "Kali couldn't take it."

I raised my chin. "Well, I can."

"That's what you think," said Ella. "But Carla's only been playing with you so far. She didn't really think you were a threat before. But now—if she wants to, Lola, she can really make your life hell."

"I'm not afraid of Carla Santini," I said, chin still in its give-me-your-best-shot position. I believe it's important in life not to be afraid of anyone or anything, not even a bad review. "She's a teenage girl, for heaven's sake, Ella, not Lady Macbeth. There's no way I'm going to let Carla Santini keep me away from the Sidhartha concert."

"Have you listened to one word I've said?" asked Ella. She shook her head in a kind of dumbfounded way. "You know," she sighed, "sometimes I can't tell whether you're just stubborn or if you're stupid, too."

8

LADY MACBETH AT DEADWOOD HIGH

A few brave souls quietly congratulated me on my triumph over Carla Santini with a smile or a nod of the head or a quick "Nice one, Lola," but Sam Creek was the only one who made a public statement about the casting.

Sam had been out all week, but on Friday he gave me the thumbs up when I walked into math.

"The Queen's been severely wounded," Sam shouted gleefully. "May she die of serious complications."

A couple of the other kids glanced our way, but no one laughed or winked or anything like that. I could feel Carla watching us from the back of the room. She was always watching me now, even when she was talking to someone else. But she never gave any sign that she actually saw me.

My counter offensive was to pretend that it was Carla and her friends who didn't exist. I flapped my cape and laughed.

"We can only hope for the best," I said loudly, as I took my seat. My smile was sour. "I'm afraid, however, that the prognosis doesn't look too good."

Sam hooted. He may not have any friends, and he might have missed the first few days of my and Ella's punishment, but he isn't stupid. He'd noticed the way the room went quiet when I stepped through the door; he'd noticed the way none of the others greeted me; he knew that Carla was sitting behind us talking about something her father had bought her while she watched like a cat waiting for the mouse to get just a tiny bit closer.

"That's a shame," said Sam. He kind of jerked his head in the Santini direction. "You may have to hire a food taster if this keeps up."

Among the BTWs and BTRs, however, no one said a word.

And when I say they didn't say a word, I mean not a word.

It took a few days, but by Friday, when the whole school knew that I was playing Eliza Doolittle and Carla Santini was playing Mrs. Higgins, even kids who had never heard of *Pygmalion* were treating me and Ella as if we were The Invisible Girls. Silent and unsmiling, the friends, friends of friends, and would-be friends of Carla Santini passed us in the hallways, sat next to us in classes, and stood near us on the lunch line as though we had ceased to exist. And all with no outward sign of hostility or show of temper from Carla herself. There were no snide comments or dirty looks; no nasty whispers or back-stabbing attacks. She shimmered around campus like a butterfly, smiling and laughing and tossing her head as though she didn't have an enemy in the world. But she could pass within inches of me or Ella as though we were air. She could say something to the entire class, and everyone would know somehow that Ella and I weren't included because we weren't really there. I got to the point where I could almost empathize with Carla. No wonder she's the way she is, I'd think as I walked ghostlike through the corridors. She must be frustrated and bored out of her mind. That was when I began to realize that Carla Santini is as wasted in Deadwood as I am—and more or less for the same reason. My spirit and talents are too large for the confines of a suburban world, and so are Carla's.

"You almost have to admire her, don't you?" I said to Ella as we walked down the hallway together like prisoners of war being marched through the streets. "Think what she could do if she were in a position of real power."

Like me, Ella kept her eyes straight ahead of her, as though unaware of the darting looks and quivering silence that followed us wherever we went.

"She's already got more power than she should," said Ella. "If it gets any colder, we're going to have to wear thermals to school."

"Oh please . . . ," I pleaded. "These are humans, not ants." In my experience, human group actions tend to fall apart eventually. "It can't last."

Ella gave me a look. "Yes, it can. This is all Carla's doing, and it won't be over till she says so."

I laughed again, this time heartily.

"Give me a break, will you? Who is Carla, Stalin? What's she going to do when people get tired of acting like jerks and start talking to us again, send them to Siberia?"

Ella nodded vehemently. "That's right. She'll send them to Siberia—with us."

I shook my head as we came to a stop outside the auditorium. "She can't," I said, dragging reason in on my side. "Carla Santini herself is going to have to start talking to me in a few minutes." The rehearsals were beginning that afternoon. Which was one of the reasons I'd been able to take the Big Freeze with a certain amount of humor. There really was no way it could last. "And when she does, everybody else will give up with relief."

Ella readjusted her book bag. "Carla won't give up," said Ella grimly. "The only thing Carla Santini's ever given up on is the concept of letting someone else have their way."

I, however, was optimistic as I walked into the auditorium by myself. Carla might have been waging a cold war against me during every other minute of the day, but she would have to leave her weapons outside the theater. The way I saw it, that was the rule. Inside, we were part of the same team. A nation divided against itself must perish; and so would the cast of *Pygmalion*.

I paused with my hand on the door. Through the thick metal I could hear the rest of the cast reading through the revised script and chatting aimlessly while they waited for the rehearsal to begin. I ruffled my hair for that urgent, passionate look, and flung my cape casually over one shoulder.

The silence of the Apocalypse fell over the room as I opened the door. All but a few people were pretending to look through their scripts or brush dirt from their shoes, as if they didn't know I'd arrived. The rest were watching me and watching Carla at the same time, waiting to see what was going to happen.

Carla Santini hadn't left her weapons in her locker, as she should have.

She was sitting in the front row, looking at Mrs. Baggoli's revisions. I could tell from the set of her back that she was fully armed.

I called out a general "Hi!"

There were a few brave mumbles in return.

I came to a stop at the front row. Carla was in an aisle seat, deeply absorbed in what she was reading. I couldn't back down. One way or another, I was going to make her talk to me.

"Hi, Carla," I said, as though these weren't the first words I'd said to her in days. I threw myself into the seat across the aisle from hers. "All ready to start?"

Carla Santini is not a great actor—she's too self-absorbed for that—but she is a good one. She did the best impersonation of a stone wall I'd ever seen.

Glances were furtively exchanged throughout our audience.

"What do you think of Mrs. Baggoli's changes?" I asked with so much good humor and interest that I should have been given an Oscar.

Carla looked up then.

But not at me. Carla looked at Andy, the boy who was playing Colonel Pickering.

"I wonder what's keeping Mrs. Baggoli," said Carla, sounding so concerned you would have thought there was a good chance that Mrs. Baggoli had been ambushed by guerrillas in the English wing.

Andy blinked. It took him a second to realize that Carla was asking him a question. She didn't normally speak to Andy; he's overweight and has acne. He looked around uneasily, a drowning man desperately searching for a passing log. Jon, who was playing Professor Higgins, rolled his eyes toward the gods. Everyone else was even less helpful; they looked away.

I raised my voice, just a little. "I saw her heading toward the office after last class."

Catlike, Carla kept her eyes on Andy, waiting for him to answer.

Andy had gone from uneasiness to a kind of mild terror. You could practically hear his palms sweating. He glanced at me, and then turned back to Carla.

"She went to the office after her last class," said Andy. He twitched, trying to decide whether or not he could safely move away now.

He couldn't.

"But school ended half an hour ago." Carla tilted her head to one side. "It isn't like Mrs. Baggoli to be late for rehearsals. Especially not the first one."

Andy stared back at her, looking as if he might implode. "Well . . . uh . . . ," he grunted.

"She had some Xeroxing she had to do," I went on, warming to my story. "For us. She has a last-minute change to the script."

Andy shifted from one foot to the other. "She's Xeroxing," he informed Carla. "You know, a last-minute change to the script."

The delicate, sculpted nostrils twitched.

"What changes? I discussed the revisions with her during lunch period, and she didn't say anything about more changes."

Andy gulped under the interrogation-strength beam of Carla's gaze.

"Oh." He looked at me out of the corners of his eyes. By now everyone else was looking at me, too.

I truly believe that if you have a good, brave heart, the forces of the universe will help you if they can. Even though the forces of the universe had been unable to keep me out of a world that includes Carla Santini, at that moment, they were able to do something else. They inspired me.

"She only thought of it last period," I said. "But she believes it could revitalize the entire play."

Andy started to relax a little.

"It was sudden," he said. "But it's big."

"Oh, really?" drawled Carla. "And just what is this big idea?"

I dropped my cape from my shoulders and leaned back in my seat.

"She's writing out Mrs. Higgins," I said with a smile.

Totally forgetting that I no longer existed, Carla turned to me, her face full of scorn. "Oh, hahaha."

I grinned. I'd known I could make her talk to me.

Not that I actually heard her—everyone else was laughing too loudly.

9
YOU CAN CHOOSE YOUR ENEMIES, BUT NOT YOUR RELATIVES

What with starting to learn the new script and being distracted because Ella and I were deep in Siberia, I hadn't yet addressed the problem of convincing my mother to let me go to New York to see Sidhartha. I was so cheered by my victory in the skirmish with Carla that afternoon, however, that I decided to launch my campaign that very night.

I know my mother; she can be handled, but it usually takes some time, and I couldn't afford to blow it because I'd waited too long to start on her. Now it was even more important that Ella and I get to the concert than it would have been normally; this had grown beyond a personal desire and become a righteous cause. I couldn't let Carla humiliate and ridicule us; I had to go to that party and laugh in her face. I owed it to the rest of the school.

It may seem naive, but I didn't really think that persuading my mother was going to be this incredibly huge problem. After all, she'd already more or less said maybe. Well, what she'd actually said was "I'll think about it." But I am destined to be a great actor. What's another thing that separates a great actor from an average one? The ability to *convince*. Convince the audience that you're an old woman when you're only in your twenties. Convince them that you're a murderer when you're really mild as a newborn lamb. Convince them that you're a saint when you're really Carla Santini.

I took the job of convincing my mother to let me go to the concert as a professional challenge. And I was confident that once Karen Kapok had given her permission, the Gerards, with their new, guilty understanding of all she'd suffered, would let Ella go, too.

"Is there something wrong with the spaghetti?" asked my mother.

She'd finally noticed. I couldn't believe it. I'd been sitting there for at least fifteen minutes, languidly pushing my food around my plate and (as usual) no one had paid me the tiniest bit of attention. The twins (also as usual) had been talking nonstop since we sat down, and whenever they paused for air or to stuff something in their mouths, my mother took up the slack, yapping on about earth-shattering things like the phone bill and the noise in the car, totally ignoring my pale, sad, silent visage on the other side of the table.

I gave my mother a wan smile.

"No," I said softly. "No, there's nothing wrong with the spaghetti." I gave her another wan smile. "I guess I'm just not very hungry." I pushed my plate away. "I guess I'm just in too much pain."

"Cramps?" asked my mother.

It seemed to me that I was always gaping at my mother in horror lately.

"Mommmm . . . ," I moaned. Ella's mother would never discuss cramps at the table in front of everybody, even though the only people usually at the Gerard's dinner table are she and Ella. Ella learned about sex and stuff like that from a book her parents gave her. It was made up of questions and answers, so she didn't have to talk about it with her mother at all.

"I'm in pain, too," said Pam. She opened her mouth as wide as she could and shoved her face in mine. "See?" she demanded. "My tooth's coming out."

All I could see was half-chewed spaghetti. It was enough to make you gag.

My mother didn't notice that one of her children was making a revolting spectacle of herself any more than she'd noticed my haunted air.

She reached for the salad. "Well?" she persisted. "There's ibuprofen in the bathroom if you need it."

"It's not that kind of pain," I said flatly.

"What kind of pain is it?" asked Paula.

I smiled at her kindly. Even though Pam and Paula are identical twins, Paula sometimes shows signs of being an intelligent life form.

"I think you're too little to understand," I gently explained. "It's a pain of the heart."

Paula sucked a strand of spaghetti into her mouth. "You mean like indigestion?"

And at other times, the closest Paula gets to an intelligent life form is sitting next to me.

"No," I said. "Not like indigestion. Like having your heart ripped from your body and thrown onto a pile of rusting tin cans. Like having a red-hot corkscrew twisted into your soul. Like having everything you ever loved or dreamed of rolled over by tanks driven by soldiers who are laughing and singing songs."

Paula looked at my mother. "What's she talking about?"

My mother shrugged. "You've got me." She helped herself to garlic bread.

"Maybe it's a bad-hair day," Pam suggested.

The twins thought this was incredibly funny. Half-chewed spaghetti and bread flew across the table.

"Girls," said my mother, but she was looking at me. "What happened?" she asked. "Are you having some trouble at school?"

"School?" I covered my heart with my hands as though I were trying to keep it from being ripped from my body yet again. "How can you talk about something as trivial as school at a time like this?" Hot, bitter tears sprang to my eyes. "Can't you see that my whole world has been pitched into darkness? Can't you see that I've lost all reason to live?"

"Are you going to tell me what happened?" asked my mother.

"That's what I mean about this family," I wailed. "Something like this can occur, and you don't even know about it."

"Well, maybe if you told us," said Paula.

I pushed back my chair. "Do you all live in a cave or something?" I shrieked. "Am I being raised by wolves? Doesn't anybody but me keep any contact with the outside world?" I got to my feet. "Sidhartha has broken up," I sobbed. "They're having one last concert at Madison Square Garden, and then they are no more!" I raised my eyes to the heavens and opened my arms. "Good night, sweet princes, may choirs of rock angels sing you to your sleep!"

Pam slurped at a forkful of food.

My mother looked at me.

"Let me make a wild guess," she said. "You want to go to the concert."

Hope dried the tears that blurred my eyes.

"Yes," I snuffled. "If I could see them play live, at least I'd have that memory to carry me through the long, empty years that lie ahead of me like a road in Kansas."

"You mean go with your dad?" asked my mother.

Good God! I'd forgotten about him. There was no way I could involve my father in this outing.

For one thing, Ella thought he was dead; for another, he was the last person we needed with us when we crashed the party.

"Dad?" I moaned with the suffering of the misunderstood. "I can't go to a Sidhartha concert with my father. I'd die of shame."

"Well, you're not going to Madison Square Garden by

yourself, and that's final," my mother informed me. "You can watch the show on MTV."

But I wasn't defeated—not yet.

"How can you treat me like this?" I cried. "I'm your flesh and blood, your first born. You used to lean over my crib in the middle of the night to make sure I was still breathing."

"Exactly," said my mother. "I'm concerned for your welfare. You can't go."

I tried to make a deal. "I'll baby-sit whenever you want for the next six months," I promised. "Free. Just let me go to the concert. *Please . . .*"

But would Karen Kapok relent? Do bears drive Volvos?

"Get off your knees, Mary," said my mother. "You can't go into the city at night by yourself and that's the end of it. The answer is no."

It was worse than mere mortal insensitivity. It was inhuman stubbornness.

What could one broken-hearted teenager do in the face of such parental pig-headedness? Sulking wouldn't work. I once stayed in my room for a whole week (except for meals, baths, going to school, and hanging out with Ella) and she didn't even notice. The silent treatment wouldn't work either. I used the silent treatment when I used the week-long sulk. All that happened was that every so often my mother would look up from whatever she was doing and comment on how nice and quiet it was for a change.

"Please," I begged. "If you don't let me go, I'll die. I swear I will. I'll just wither away and die."

"Well, if you ask me, that's better than being shot at close range by some psycho in Manhattan," said my mother.

My chair toppled over as, devastated, I fled from the room.

"If Mary dies, can we have the porch as a playroom?" asked Pam.

"Can you believe it?" I complained to Ella the next day as we walked to homeroom. "I live in a house without pity, in a cheap temple to the meaningless frivolity of contemporary life." I flapped my arms so my cape moved like wings. "She wouldn't even listen to me, Ella. She wouldn't even stop for one tiny little nanosecond and consider me. My feelings. My needs. My fragile hopes and dreams. Me! Her oldest child, the child of the only man she ever really loved."

Ella gave me a darting glance. "That means you asked your mother about the concert and she said no, doesn't it?"

There was something about her tone that I didn't like. A smugness. If Ella weren't raised to be so polite and pleasant all the time, she would have stuck out her tongue and said, "Nahnahnah, I told you so!"

"Well, at least I asked," I snapped. "At least I made the attempt, instead of just throwing up my hands in defeat." I raised my chin to the winter sun. "At least I do battle, Ella."

"I asked," said Ella quietly. "I asked them days ago."

I came to an abrupt halt and stared at her as though I'd never seen her before. It may not sound like a big deal to anyone with parents less dedicated to perfection than Ella's, but this kind of behavior is unheard of in the Gerard household. Not only do the Gerards never argue, never shout, and never behave like their brains are asleep, they achieve this amazing state of perfection by avoiding even the most everyday confrontations. It's kind of an unwritten rule that Ella never says or does anything to upset her parents. She does whatever they want automatically, and— consciously or subconsciously—doesn't do things they wouldn't want.

"Really?" I couldn't have hidden my surprise if I'd wanted to. The more I knew Ella, the more I realized there was more to know. "You actually asked Marilyn and Jim if you can go into New York, the evil heart of the universe, and see Sidhartha? You admitted that there are things that you'd rather do than watch videos and go to the mall?" Watching videos and shopping— two things that drive Karen Kapok wild if done to excess—are considered appropriate teenage pursuits by the Gerards.

Ella nodded. "Uh huh. Well, I asked my mother." She kind of shrugged with her mouth. "I never manage to stay up late enough to see my father most of the time."

"And what did she say?"

Ella made a face. "She said no."

I sighed and started walking again. "That, of course, was to be expected," I said. "But I really thought my mother would come around. After all, I can understand your mother worrying about you. You've never even been on a subway. But me? I know my way around The City like a rat. My mother has nothing to worry about."

"What does it matter?" asked Ella. "We can't go, and that's the end of it."

But I am not a "Que será, será" kind of person.

"No, it isn't," I informed her. "It's just the beginning."

10

THE THAW

It wasn't as if Carla Santini exactly surrendered and signed the peace treaty after I confronted her in that first rehearsal. She pretended I was human when Mrs. Baggoli was around and ignored me as much as she could whenever Mrs. Baggoli was out of the room. But she had other ways of getting revenge.

Mrs. Baggoli clapped her hands together. "Let's have some quiet in here!" she shouted. "Higgins, Mrs. Pearce, Eliza . . . let's try it one more time." She pointed at me. "Start with 'Don't I look dumb?'"

I nodded. I raised my head. "Don't I look dumb?"

"Dumb?" asked Professor Higgins.

"Mrs. Baggoli," said Carla Santini. "I'm sorry to interrupt again, but do you really think *dumb*'s the right word?"

Mrs. Baggoli doesn't tolerate rudeness or dissension among her cast, so no one groaned out loud the way they would have normally; but we all shot desperate looks at one another. It wasn't so much that Carla interrupted *us;* it was more like we interrupted *her.*

Mrs. Baggoli sighed. She knew that she couldn't yell

at Carla because Carla wasn't really doing anything wrong. She wasn't goofing off or snickering in the background or anything like that. She was just trying to make sure that everything—and everyone—was as good as it could be. I know this because it was something Carla said at every rehearsal, at least once, usually when Mrs. Baggoli's awesome patience was about to snap in two.

"Carla," said Mrs. Baggoli very slowly and distinctly, "we all appreciate your sense of perfection about this production, but it really would be helpful if we could get through at least one whole scene this afternoon."

She could have added, "For a change," but she didn't.

Carla wrung her manicured hands. "Oh, I know, I know," she said, her voice tormented and deeply apologetic. How could anyone be mad at her when she was suffering so nobly for all our sakes? "I know I'm being a nuisance, but this is so important to me—"

Mrs. Baggoli put up one hand. "Please," she pleaded. "It's important to all of us. Maybe you could just save all your questions till we're through."

Carla nodded. "Of course," she said. "Of course you're right. I'll wait until we're through."

"Okay." Mrs. Baggoli took a deep breath. "Once more, Eliza."

If we'd been making a film instead of rehearsing a play, at that point someone would have jumped in front of us with a clapboard and screamed, "*Pygmalion*. Act Two, take sixteen."

We started yet again. This time we got as far as Eliza telling Higgins that her father only came to get some money to get drunk with when Carla's calfskin shoulder bag crashed to the floor.

Everyone looked at Carla.

"I'm so sorry . . . ," crooned Carla as she picked her bag from the floor. "I was looking for a pen and paper so I could write down my questions."

"I have an idea," said Mrs. Baggoli. "Why don't we run through the beginning of Act Three instead?"

Mrs. Baggoli might be a little naive and too patient for her own good, and she had no idea what was really going on, but she isn't a fool. Act Three featured Mrs. Higgins. By now all of us knew that the only way you could get Carla to shut up when I was on-stage and she wasn't was to change the scene.

You could hear a sigh that was half relief and half frustration ripple through the auditorium.

"Jesus, we're going to have to start rehearsing our scenes in secret," Professor Higgins muttered as Carla got out of her seat.

Colonel Pickering snorted.

Personally, I wouldn't have minded rehearsing every scene in secret, especially the ones where Carla and I appeared together. When we were on together, she did everything in her power to throw me off or steal my scene. She'd change lines, she'd forget to cue me, or she'd stand in such a way that the only thing anyone in the audience could see was the top of my head.

Both Professor Higgins and Colonel Pickering smiled as though their dearest wish had just come true when Carla pranced onto the stage. Nobody said anything to Carla's face that wasn't a compliment. Not and lived to tell the tale.

It's true that—except for Carla, who addressed me stiffly, if I were sitting on her coat or something—everyone in the cast was friendly toward me from then on, but outside rehearsals the Big Freeze continued for weeks. Only in math, where Sam Creek made a point of talking to me at length about the intricacies of the internal combustion engine, was there any kind of warmth.

Ella and I were getting oddly used to the Big Freeze, to tell you the truth. In fact, Ella said that she almost enjoyed it because it took all the stress and strain out of having to be interested and friendly to people you felt neither interested in nor particularly friendly toward. Since I have never felt the same obligation as Ella to be nice to absolutely everybody, I didn't feel the same relief, but I actually didn't mind it either.

And then, as suddenly as the explosion of a terrorist bomb, things changed.

We were walking to our first class, and Tina Cherry smiled at us as she passed with a pack of her lesser friends. Because Tina smiled, the rest of them smiled, too.

Again, this doesn't sound like a big deal. So some girl

you've seen practically every school day for the last year smiles at you, so what? So something had happened, that's so what. Tina did what Carla Santini did, or what Carla Santini told her to do. If Tina was smiling, something was up.

"I wonder what brought that on," I mused, glancing over my shoulder to make sure that Tina wasn't sneaking up behind us, brandishing a knife. I'd read my Shakespeare. I knew all about the daggers in men's smiles.

"I don't know, but I don't like it," said Ella.

We turned the corner and walked into Marcia Conroy and her boyfriend of the week. Carla Santini and her friends go through guys the way someone with a bad cold goes through tissues. What gets me is that even though everybody knows this, there's always another guy right behind the last one, waiting to be picked up and dumped in almost one swift movement.

"Lola," purred Marcia. "Ella." She stretched her mouth in a mirthless kind of way.

We strode past her without a glance.

"Something's definitely up," said Ella. "I just wish we knew what."

"I'm sure we'll find out soon," I assured her. "Carla, like God, may work in mysterious ways, but she doesn't have God's patience."

An observation that turned out to be prophetic.

Carla decided to sit near us at lunch.

"I've been looking all over for you two," she boomed, catching the attention of anyone who could hear. She dumped her stuff on the table behind us.

Ella froze in mid-bite, gazing at Carla over her forkful of pasta salad. Everyone else was gazing at Carla, too, but with curiosity, not horror.

I looked up. "Haven't you heard?" I asked sweetly. "You're not supposed to talk to us."

You have to hand it to Carla; she has grace under fire.

"Oh, that . . ." She waved her nails in the air. "I really don't know what that was all about."

The Big Freeze was over; Carla was speaking to us again. We were about to be engulfed in an avalanche.

Carla threw herself into the chair next to mine and started rummaging in her bag. "I knew you'd want to see this," she gushed.

The only thing Carla Santini could show me that I would want to see is a picture of the house she's moving to in Yugoslavia.

"Really?"

Carla ignored the boredom in my voice.

"Look what came in the mail for me yesterday," she ordered with girlish excitement. "They've just been printed. They won't even be going on sale for at least another week."

She was holding two rectangles of black cardboard. SIDHARTHA—*THE FAREWELL CONCERT*—PRESS was written across them in silver. She raised the tickets in the air for a few seconds so the rest of the cafeteria could admire them, too.

"And that's not all!" Carla's voice was loud enough to deafen anyone within a mile radius. "Look what else I got."

She held out a third rectangle of black cardboard. This one said SIDHARTHA'S LAST BASH, and, underneath in smaller print, the place and time and the information that it would admit two.

There was a chorus of "Wow"s around us. A couple of people crowded closer for a better view.

"God, you're lucky," said one of the onlookers, a girl whom, normally, Carla would never have noticed. "Imagine going to a party like that."

Carla smiled on the girl, the queen among the peasants.

"Oh, but I'm not the only one," cooed Carla. "Lola has an invitation, too." I flinched as she put a hand on my shoulder. "Don't you, Lola?"

I didn't answer. I was still staring at her invitation, imprinting the address on my brain before she put it away.

Carla made a few loud gestures of shock and outrage. "Don't tell me you haven't gotten yours yet," she cried. "Stu told my father that they'd all gone out."

I didn't believe this for one fraction of a nano-second. Like Stu Wolff had dropped everything else in his life to make sure Mr. Santini knew how the plans for the party were going. Yeah, right . . .

"I didn't say I didn't get my invitation." I gave Carla a tolerant and amused smile. "As a matter of fact, mine came yesterday."

"Well, show it to us," said Carla. Her eyes flitted over our audience. "I'm sure I'm not the only one who'd like to see it."

I laughed as though she'd suggested that I wear my diamonds to school. "I'm not bringing it *here.*"

Carla's smile locked on me like a clamp. "Oh, come on, Lola," she coaxed. "Why don't you just admit that you don't have one and get it over with? It'll save you a lot of humiliation later on."

I counter-clamped. "I'm sure there'll be lots of photographers at the party," I said. "Maybe we can have our picture taken together."

"It's a deal," said Carla. She turned to face Ella for the first time. "You know," she went on, gently waving the invitation in the air over our table, "this *does* admit two, El. If you really want to go you could always come with me."

Behind me, Alma gasped in surprise. She was obviously under the impression that she was going with Carla. But she didn't so much as bleat in protest—she never dares to opens her mouth unless it's to agree.

"Thanks, but no thanks," said Ella loyally. "I'm sure I'll see you there."

11

DESPERATE MEASURES FOR DESPERATE TIMES

"Maybe moving's not such a bad idea," said Ella on the phone that afternoon. "I mean, unless Carla suddenly contracts some rare but fatal disease and dies, there really isn't any other solution."

My mother was in her studio, working on a rush order, and the twins were over at a friend's for supper, so for a change I had a little privacy while I conversed.

"Of course there's another solution," I said with a certain amount of exasperation.

"Murder's out of the question," said Ella primly. "I don't like violence."

I laughed. "Don't worry, I'm not going to jail for Carla Santini. All we have to do is what I've been saying all along; beat her at her own game."

Ella's voice flattened. "You mean go to the party."

"Well, of course I mean go to the party," I shrieked. "You seemed to agree with me at lunch."

"I was acting," said Ella. "Remember acting?"

"We have to go," I insisted. "This clinches it."

"We can't go," replied Ella. "You're just going to have to live with that fact."

But I didn't want to live with that fact.

"Don't you see," I pleaded. "I can't let Carla Santini get the better of me, El. Not now. Not when she's finally on the run."

"Carla doesn't run anywhere," said Ella. "She drives."

"Ella, be reasonable. If she's decided to be all nice again, it's because she's planning to wipe the courtyard with us later. You're the one who's always saying how dangerous she is. Well, if she's that dangerous, we have to stop her."

"So what are you going to do?" Ella demanded. "You heard Carla. The tickets go on sale next week."

I stared at the bowl of fruit on the kitchen table, like a pagan priest staring at a steaming heap of sheep intestine, looking for the answer. And it worked. Just as the priest would see the future in the bleeding innards, I saw the future in the dusty apples and bananas. I smiled to myself. Desperate measures for desperate times. . . .

"I'm going to go on a hunger strike."

"You really are crazy," said Ella. "You really and truly are."

"No I'm not. Passive resistance works, El. Look at Gandhi. Look at Martin Luther King."

"They were both assassinated," said Ella.

I sighed. Sometimes she can be as stubborn as my mother.

"That was afterward. After their methods had worked."

"Okay," said Ella. "What about Bobby Sands?"

I knew this was a trick question, but I said, "Who?" anyway.

"Bobby Sands," Ella repeated. "He was in prison for IRA activities, and he went on a hunger strike against the British government."

I took a wild guess. "It didn't work?"

"Not exactly," said Ella. "He starved to death."

Even though she couldn't see me, I threw up my arms.

"Well, that's not going to happen to me, is it?" I demanded.

"You mean because your mother will put you in the hospital and have you force-fed?"

I laughed heartily. "Of course not. Because I'm not going to stop eating. I'm just going to make her think that I have."

My mother doesn't alphabetize the canned and packaged foods the way Ella's mother does, and our refrigerator doesn't look like a display model when you open it up with an orderly and attractive assortment of fruits, vegetables, and juices inside. Our fridge is filled with spoonfuls of this and dollops of that in bowls my mother couldn't sell, a few bendable carrots, and a couple of bottles of juice with bits of food floating in them because the twins never bother using glasses. But I knew my mother would still know if anything was missing. I blame her occupation. She has an eye for detail.

So the next afternoon after rehearsal, I stopped at the supermarket and filled my book bag with supplies: cheese, apples, crackers, a couple of containers of salads and juices, a jar of pickles, and a box of doughnuts. I figured that should get me through supper and breakfast.

I hid everything in different places in my room, just to be on the safe side. In her one-woman war on dirt and disorder, Ella's mother goes through Ella's room with the thoroughness of a policeman searching for evidence, but my mother doesn't mind a little dirt and disorder, especially if it isn't hers and the door is kept shut. On the other hand, although my father would believe I was doing what I'd said I was doing—fasting—my mother was almost certain to be suspicious. This was partly because she's been feeding me since I was born and knows how much I like food, and partly because she has a skeptical nature. I think this is because she's a woman. In my experience, women are a lot less trusting than men.

I hid the cheese under the pile of shoes on the floor of my closet; the fruit under my papier-mâché bust of Shakespeare; the crackers behind my dresser; the pickles at the bottom of my dirty-clothes basket; the salads behind my bookcase; and the juices under my bed. Then I put on a Sidhartha album, lit some candles, and lay down to wait for the clarion cry that signified supper.

It was Paula who called me.

"Mary!" she shrieked through the door. "Mary, Mom says to come and eat!"

"Tell her, if I can't go to the Sidhartha concert, I'm never eating again," I shouted back.

She returned in under a minute.

"Mom says to come out now," bellowed Paula.

"I told you," I screamed. "I'm not eating. Not now, not tomorrow, not ever!"

"If you're not eating, can I have your dessert?" asked Paula.

"Have my dessert, have my supper, have anything you want."

I could hear Paula shouting as she went back to the kitchen, "Mary says I can have her dessert."

The next person at my door was Karen Kapok herself. Banging.

"What's going on?" demanded my mother.

"I'm on a hunger strike," I screamed back over Stu Wolff singing, "No more . . . no more . . . I've found the door. . . ." "I'm like Gandhi, driven to desperate measures by the insensitivity of the British government. Not one morsel will pass my lips until you say I can go see Sidhartha."

"You have two minutes to get to the table," said my mother. "If you don't, the insensitive British government is going to take your door off its hinges and drag you out."

* * *

You have to appreciate the way an unimaginative, practical mind like my mother's works. She thought that if I was forced to sit through every meal, watching the rest of them feeding, hunger would overcome my iron resolve, and I would give in.

Ignoring my pale skin and the dark circles under my eyes, she made me sit through every meal.

At first my mother kept asking me to pass her stuff: "Mary, could you please pass the salad? . . . Mary, would you please pass the salt? . . . Would you mind passing the vegetables, Mary?"

When my mother wasn't asking me to hand her every edible item on the table, she was oohing and ahhing over every atom that touched her lips.

The twins were even less subtle. They kept waving pieces of food in my face and shrieking, "Don't you want some, Mare? It's *really* good."

Recalling my Joan of Arc phase, I refused to be tempted, responding to the crass coercion of my family with stoic dignity and grace.

"Of course," I'd say every time my mother asked for something. I'd smile gently as though it pleased me that her appetite was so healthy. "No, thank you," I'd whisper whenever Pam or Paula shoved a piece of garlic bread or a cookie in my nose.

On Friday, my mother brought in the heavy artillery: she made lasagna, my most favorite dish in the entire universe. Just the smell of it nearly made me swoon.

But I was strong and resolute, and full of doughnuts, so her strategy didn't work.

Great actors know what real determination and dedication are. Ordinary people, however, do not. They give up easily. By breakfast on Saturday my family had gone back to totally ignoring me as usual. They munched away at their pancakes, all three of them talking at the same time, as if a victim of oppression and injustice weren't sitting among them, staring at her empty plate, as isolated from their food and trivial chitchat as a prisoner in a Mexican jail.

I took this, of course, as a good sign. The twins were already bored with the game, and my mother, also bored with the game, had obviously decided that I'd give up if I didn't get any attention. My mother's understanding of the psychology of the gifted is pretty limited.

I wouldn't give up. I would step up my resistance instead.

I sipped my glass of water and smiled at them wanly all through the meal, and when it was over, I said I was going back to bed because I was feeling so tired.

I spent Saturday languishing in my room. I managed to stagger out to sip my water while they stuffed their faces with supper, but a sudden wave of dizziness forced me to leave the table halfway through. "I'm sorry," I whispered apologetically, "but I'm too weak to sit here. I have to lie down."

I was still languishing on Sunday. By then, of course,

I was too weak and exhausted to come out to watch them eat breakfast.

"I can't," I called hoarsely through my closed bedroom door. "The room spins whenever I stand up."

My mother was her usual cynical self.

"Why don't you just crawl out, then?" she shouted back.

My father called that afternoon, but I was too weak to make it to the phone. By putting a glass to my door and my ear to the glass, I could just make out my mother explaining to my father that she was starving me to death.

"She's doing Gandhi this week," said my mother. "She's on a hunger strike until I say she can go to some concert at the Garden."

There were a few minutes of silence then while my father talked.

Although my father's speciality is adorable rabbits, he is technically an artist. This makes him more sensitive and compassionate than my mother, the pot maker. My father would never be able to watch me waste away before his eyes the way my mother was. I had my hopes pinned on him.

Finally, my mother spoke.

"I'll ask her," she said. I could tell from her voice that she thought my father was being too soft. She always thinks my father's being too soft. Attila the Hun would have seemed soft to my mother. "Mary!" she called. She put down the receiver and started walking toward my door.

I flung myself back into bed, jamming the glass under the pillow.

"Mary!" my mother called again. "Mary, your dad has an idea. . . ."

My dad's idea was that he take me to the concert and I spend the night with him.

This wasn't the idea I wanted him to have. I wanted him to have the idea that I was mature and responsible enough to go by myself.

"Oh ye gods . . . ," I moaned. "Isn't it enough that you've practically killed me? Now you want to humiliate me, too?"

"Well, what about this?" asked my mother. "What if Cal takes you to the Garden and then picks you up when the concert's over?"

"What?" I shrieked. "Like a little kid being picked up from the day care center? Is there no end to the shame you want to heap on me?"

"Suit yourself," said my mother. She went back to the phone. She told my dad that I'd rejected his offer.

"Oh, for God's sake, Cal," snapped my mother. "It's been a couple of days, not six months. She's fine." She was silent for a few minutes and then she screamed, "Mary! Your father wants to talk to you!"

"I told you!" I rasped back. "I can't get out of bed. My legs are too weak to hold me up."

"She's dying," said my mother. "She can't come to the phone right now."

My father called at least two more times that afternoon. He must have gotten my mother worried, though, because when I didn't come out for supper, she finally cracked.

She marched into my room with a plate of food in her hands. I didn't even try to lift my head from the pillow. A person melting away from hunger loses her natural curiosity.

"This has gone far enough," announced my mother. "I want to talk to you."

My mother said that she couldn't stand by and watch me fade away before her eyes. What kind of mother was she if she let one of her children make herself ill? She would never be able to live with herself if something happened to me. And there was also my father to consider. He was very upset. I knew how emotional he was, how stressed and pressured he was with work and everything. What was I trying to do, push him into an early crematorium?

"You're going to eat tonight, or I'm going to know the reason why," my mother concluded.

The long days of starvation made it hard for me to speak.

"The reason why," I croaked, "is because I'm on a hunger strike." I turned my haunted eyes on her. "Passive resistance," I whispered. My mother is big on passive resistance; her brother spent the Vietnam War in jail.

"A rock concert is not worth starvation," said my

mother. She put the plate on the bed and helped me to sit up. Then she picked up the plate again and put it in front of me. "Now, eat," she ordered.

"I can't," I said in a choked voice.

My mother folded her arms. "Oh, yes you can."

I glanced behind her. The twins were hovering in the doorway, devouring corn bread and giggling in their usual childish manner.

"Make them go away," I begged.

My mother looked over her shoulder. "Go back to the table!" she commanded.

Pam spit a mouthful of corn bread down her shirt, but otherwise my sisters didn't move.

I picked up my fork. Hesitatingly, as though I'd forgotten how to use silverware. I slipped my fork into the mashed potato on my plate. I raised a small morsel to my lips. I paused.

"Eat it," my mother commanded.

I slid the fork into my mouth. But my poor, frail body was unused to rich things like mashed potato with mushroom gravy—I started to gag.

"Mary's throwing up!" shrieked Pam. "Mary's throwing up on her bed!"

"Oh, how gross," squealed Paula.

My mother lost a little of her compassionate manner.

"Mary can't be throwing up," she assured them. "She hasn't eaten anything in nearly three days. Remember? "

"Mom's right," I gasped. I figured that since I had an

audience, I might as well play to them. "I'm just tearing my empty stomach apart." Choking so much I was turning red, I spat the potato back on my plate.

"Why do I feel like I'm watching a tragedy in one act?" asked my mother.

Still choking, I started to cry.

"Make her eat more," pleaded Pam. "I want to see her throw up again."

"Is Mary going to die?" asked Paula.

My mother's brows were knit.

"It smells like something has died in here," she said.

I peeked through my tears and sobs to find her looking around suspiciously, her nose twitching.

"Am I the only one who smells that?" she demanded.

Paula and Pam hurled themselves into my room.

"Peeoiu!" they shrieked, holding their noses.

"It smells like rotten eggs," said my mother.

"It smells like it's coming from the bed," said Paula.

It was rotten eggs. And it was coming from around the bed. Saturday morning, Ella had brought me some leftovers from her supper the night before and I'd stuck the plate under the bed because I wasn't hungry then. I'd totally forgotten about it.

My mother dove under the bed like a beagle, and, like a beagle, came up with the remains of Mrs. Gerard's mushroom quiche. She looked at it for a few seconds and then she looked at me.

That was my cue.

I pretended to faint.

12

OUR MINOR DETAILS GROW

Despite my unexpected setback with passive resistance, I was in a good mood on Monday.

Indeed, I was more than happy; I was ecstatic. George Blue made the announcement Saturday night: Monday was the day the tickets to the Sidhartha concert went on sale.

"I'll tell Mrs. Baggoli I have bad cramps and can't make rehearsal today," I was saying to Ella as we walked to class. It was a big chance to take, missing rehearsal. Carla Santini was my understudy, after all. It made me nervous, her playing my part. But it was a chance I would have to take. "Then right after school we'll go to the mall and get our tickets." I spread my arms, and the black velvet fluttered like a raven's wings. "I'm practically dancing in Stu Wolff's embrace."

"Lola," said Ella. "Lola, it may have slipped your mind, but neither of us has permission to go to the concert."

"Details, details," I cried as we turned into the English wing. "I'll just tell my mom I'm spending the night with you, and you'll tell your parents you're spending the night with me." I snapped my fingers. "What could be easier?" It seemed pretty foolproof to me.

But it didn't seem that foolproof to Ella.

"It won't work," Ella said flatly. She swung her book bag back and forth between us in a resigned way. "You know what my mother's like. She's guaranteed to call your house at least once to make sure I didn't forget anything."

Sadly, I did know what Ella's mother was like. Mrs. Gerard still reminds Ella to brush her teeth. I mean, really. Ella's sixteen. Was her mother going to move in to Ella's dorm when she went to college so she could remind her to brush her teeth every night then, too?

"Okay," I said reasonably. "Then we'll tell them the truth."

Ella gave me a sour look.

"The truth? You want to tell them that we're going to go to the Sidhartha concert, and then we're going to crash a party where everyone will probably be drunk or on drugs and making out in the bathroom?"

I sighed. "Not that truth. We'll tell them we're going to the concert, but that we're going with my friend Shana and that her folks are going to meet us at the train and escort us to the Garden." Shana was the friend I told Ella I was seeing when I visited my father. I really did visit Shana when I first moved to Deadwood, but we'd drifted apart, as people do.

"Um . . . ," said Ella.

"And we'll tell them we're going to spend the night

with her," I went on. "Her parents have been married for twenty-five years. Your parents will like that."

"Lola," said Ella in this megapatient voice. "What if—"

"Stop worrying," I advised. I opened the classroom door. "So we still have a few minor details to work out."

Ella snorted. If her mother could have heard her, she would have gone into cardiac arrest. God only has ten commandments, but Mrs. Gerard has at least a hundred, a great many of them pertaining to proper behavior for young ladies.

"You can say that again," said Ella. She glanced toward the back of the room, the new location for the Carla Santini Admiration Society. "More than a few."

Right on cue, Carla Santini looked over.

"Lola and Ella are going, too," she boomed as we took our seats.

You didn't have to be particularly gifted as a detective to correctly guess what Carla was droning on about. Even though everybody, including the janitor, knew the whole saga of the Sidhartha concert, including every word that had ever been exchanged between Stu Wolff and Mr. Santini, it was a routine Carla never tired of.

"Lola's mother, the potter, got them invited."

"She must be a pretty good potter," said one of the boys in Carla's audience.

They all laughed, even Carla, who had made that same dumb joke herself.

I was getting pretty good at duplicating Carla's smile.

"As good a potter as Mr. Santini is a lawyer," I said, joining in the laughter.

"Suicide," hissed Ella. "You're committing high-school suicide."

Alma could do a pretty good imitation of the Santini smile, too.

"So you must be used to these celebrity gigs if your mother has clients like Marsh Foreman," she purred.

"Oh, you know . . ." I was cool, as someone a little jaded from her life in the fast lane would be.

Ella groaned.

Alma gave me a "get *you*" kind of look. "What about the concert? Are you going to that, too?"

I felt, rather than saw, Ella glance my way.

"Of course they're going," drawled Carla Santini. The dark curls rattled. "We fortunate ones with personal invitations don't have to worry about tickets to the concert, do we, Lola?"

The classroom door opened and shut, and the cavalry in the form of Mrs. Baggoli rushed in. I sat down.

"Nope," I agreed. "We fortunate ones don't have to worry about tickets."

"It's not for me," I was saying. My voice was soft and gentle, but charged with emotion and suffering. "It's for my poor sister."

Mr. Alvarez, whose nametag claimed he was the

manager of Ticketsgalore, was still shaking his head. "Well, I'm really very sorry about your sister—"

"Mary." I smiled a bittersweet smile. "You see," I whispered, leaning over the counter toward him, my eyes dark with pain, my youthful features etched with tragedy, "Mary's dying. Of a very rare blood disease."

Ella began to choke. I reached out and slapped her on the back, my eyes still on Mr. Alvarez.

Mr. Alvarez looked embarrassed. "I'm very sorry to hear that," he said quickly, "but I'm afraid—"

"Sidhartha's her very favorite band," I rushed on. "No, they're more than just a band to poor Mary. They're a source of hope and inspiration. A spiritual well in which she can dip her battered soul for nourishment and rest." My voice became a little louder with the intensity of my emotions. "Sidhartha and their music have kept her going through all she's had to endure in her tortured young life—the isolation, the operations, the coma. . . ." I clasped my hands in supplication. I stared into Mr. Alvarez's eyes. "If she could just see their last concert, she could at least die happy."

Mr. Alvarez pushed a limp strand of hair from his forehead. "I'd love to help you," he said. "I really would. It's very sad about your sister—"

"Mary," I breathed. "Her name's Mary." I smiled bravely. "She's only eighteen." I bit my lip. "Eighteen, but never nineteen."

With a sigh, Ella wandered away to check out the posters on the walls.

"Really," said Mr. Alvarez. He was almost pleading. "If there were something I could do to help you, I would. But there isn't. I simply don't have any more tickets."

I was leaning so close by now that I could smell the traces of Mr. Alvarez's lunch (fish and garlic).

"But there must be some way," I insisted, forcing back a sob. "Someone somewhere must have tickets left."

"Maybe," Mr. Alvarez conceded. He made an apologetic face. "I really wish I could help you, but I just don't have any."

A single tear slid down my careworn cheek. "Not even one?"

He shook his head again. "Not even one. If I did, believe me, I'd let you have it."

I touched his hand. "Thank you," I whispered. "God bless you. And I'm sure poor Mary would thank you if—" I paused, choked with emotion, "if she could."

Ella and I walked out of the store in silence. But as soon as the door of Ticketsgalore shut behind us, she turned on me almost hysterically.

"God bless you?" she shrieked. "My poor sister Mary's dying of a rare blood disease? She'd thank you herself if she could?" Ella looked torn between shock and awe. "I'm surprised you didn't invite him to the funeral."

I led the way to a nearby bench. "What are you getting so worked up about?" I demanded. "We would have had the tickets if he really wasn't sold out, and you know it. I bet if he had a couple put aside he would have given them to us for nothing."

"Yeah," said Ella. "Just to get rid of us."

We collapsed side by side under a palm tree. Even though it's located in the temperate northeast, for some reason the Dellwood Mall has a tropical decor.

"If my mother wasn't too cheap to let me have my own credit card, this would never have happened," I grumbled. You could bet Carla Santini had her own credit card. Undoubtedly platinum.

"It's probably for the best," said Ella, placid again. She sighed. "I don't think I could have handled all the lying involved if we really did go. Your mother . . . my parents . . ." She gave another sigh. "I've always been taught that honesty is the best policy. It's a hard habit to break."

"Well, you'd better start practicing," I informed her, my mind already steaming on to the next solution. "Because we're still going, tickets or no tickets."

Ella gave me one of her long, hard looks. "You know, it's just as well you want to be an actor," she informed me, "because you definitely have no talent for reality. Don't you get it, Lola? No ticket, no entry. That's the rule."

I gave her a withering look.

"Scalpers," I said simply. "Or, even better, we could crash the concert, too."

But Ella was shaking her head. "I can't do it, Lola, I—"

She broke off as Carla, Alma, and at least half a dozen glossy shopping bags came out of the Armani store to our left. Even though they were both talking faster than the speed of light, Carla and Alma spotted

126

us immediately—and immediately swooped toward us, smiles flashing.

"Oh no, company," muttered Ella.

The company of hyenas.

"I think I liked it better when they weren't speaking to us," I whispered.

"Well, look who's here!" boomed Carla. She gave me a low-beam smile. "I thought you were crippled with cramps."

Several passing shoppers, hearing her roar, looked over at me and Ella.

"I'm feeling better, thanks," I replied smoothly. "How come you're not at rehearsal?"

Carla's expression became serious. "Mrs. Baggoli's neighbor called just as we were starting, to say that her house alarm was going off again, so she had to go home."

"Carla and I have been doing a little shopping," said Alma. She giggled.

Carla's eyes were running over Ella and me like ants over a picnic. One eyebrow rose. "What," she grinned, her eyes resting on me, "no booty?"

I grinned back. "We just got here. You know what the buses are like."

"Oh," said Carla, who had probably never been on a bus in her life, "so that's it." She laughed loudly. "You had me worried for a minute," she went on. "I thought you must have come out of there." Her eyes darted behind me to where the neon Ticketsgalore sign shone.

"I was afraid you hadn't gotten your tickets after all." Her expression changed to one of sisterly concern. "And that would be such a shame."

"Yeah," I said. "It certainly would."

"Of course," Carla went on, "Ella doesn't have to worry. She can still come with me."

This time I could see Alma's reaction. She looked as if she'd been slapped in the face with a piece of wet seaweed. But she still didn't say anything.

Ella sighed. Whatever she'd been about to say before Carla and Alma turned up about why she couldn't go through with any of my plans was gone for good. Ella has very strong views on friendship and loyalty.

"I told you before," said Ella, sweet as a steel bar coated in honey, "I'm going with Lola."

13

I THROW MYSELF INTO THE PLAY

Since the concert was still weeks away, I gave myself body and soul to *Pygmalion*. Naturally, this helped to ease the deep pain inside me about the breakup. It also won me points with Mrs. Baggoli. She'd already congratulated me on how hard I was working. "I always knew you were right for Eliza," she'd said, "but I have to admit that you've immersed yourself in the part beyond even my expectations." The only thing it didn't do was shut Carla Santini up.

"It really is a problem," Carla Santini was saying to Colonel Pickering and the Parlor Maid. "I mean, what *does* one wear to a party like this? There are going to be so many fantastically famous people there dressing down. . . ." She glanced in my direction. "And so many hangers-on trying to dress up. . . ." Her sigh was like the sound of a nearly empty aerosol can. "I mean, I'm going to meet Stu Wolff, guaranteed. I want to make the right impression."

Stu Wolff and Carla Santini, guaranteed. I looked toward the door, hoping to see Mrs. Baggoli hurrying in with the cup of coffee she'd gone to get. The doorway was empty.

The Parlor Maid giggled. "I wish I had problems like that."

Colonel Pickering, who was obviously as tired of hearing about Carla's dress dilemma as I was, mumbled something about going over his lines again before the break was over, and drifted away.

"I was thinking I might just wear my Calvins and a silk shirt," Carla went on to the Parlor Maid, without missing a beat, "but Daddy thinks I should wear a dress. You know, because so many of these people are clients or potential clients. We do have an image to maintain." She smiled coyly. "Of course, Daddy will buy me something new. He doesn't expect me to go in just any old rags."

Heaven forbid.

I tried to shut out the sound of her voice, as annoying as the sound of a mosquito in the middle of the night. I started thinking about how unfair life is. Why should some people have so much, and others so little? Why should some people have so many teeth, expensive clothes, cell phones, and guaranteed introductions to Stu Wolff, while others sleep on the porch, have to use the family phone, and have no guarantee that they won't be arrested trying to meet Stu Wolff?

I became so involved in the incredible unfairness of it all that I didn't realize Mrs. Baggoli was back until she clapped her hands for silence.

I looked up.

"All right, everyone," shouted Mrs. Baggoli. "Break's over. Let's take it from the top again. Andy and Jon, take your places." She looked over to where Carla was standing with her face to the wall, going over her lines in a whisper that could be heard in Arkansas. "Carla!" called Mrs. Baggoli. "Carla, please get on-stage."

Carla raised her chin. She tilted her head. She told Henry Higgins to behave himself.

"Mrs. Higgins!" yelled Mrs. Baggoli. "Mrs. Higgins, will you please take your place on stage!"

Carla turned around, her beautiful face flushed with embarrassment and confusion. "Oh, I'm so sorry, Mrs. Baggoli," she gushed. "I didn't hear you. I was so wrapped up in perfecting my tone."

Although Carla acted as though this announcement was something worthy of the evening news, Mrs. Baggoli took the information in stride. Carla was still constantly perfecting something at rehearsals. If it wasn't her tone or her accent or her motivation, it was someone else's. Professor Higgins walked out once because Carla suggested that he didn't understand his own character. Personally, if she didn't stop trying to help me with my performance, I was going to have to kill her.

"Try perfecting your tone on-stage," said Mrs. Baggoli. She looked over at me as I got into position in the wings. "No script today, Lola?"

I shook my head. "I think I know it cold." I should

have. I'd been doing nothing else every night for weeks. If I hesitated over a line for a nanosecond, Carla would start hissing it at me.

Mrs. Baggoli smiled.

Carla gave me a scornful look, threw her script on a chair, and climbed up on the stage.

Today we were going through Act Five, where Henry Higgins goes to his mother's house after Eliza leaves him and discovers that she's there.

Mrs. Baggoli took a seat in the front row. "All right," she called. "Let's start where Mrs. Higgins tells Henry and Pickering why Eliza left."

Carla started off. Even I had to admit that she was a good Mrs. Higgins. Probably because they were both used to bossing the servants around. Jon started to come in too soon and cut Carla off in midsentence. She sighed and gave Mrs. Baggoli a look filled with patient suffering. Mrs. Baggoli told her to start again.

Carla started again but stopped again almost immediately. She had a question about Mrs. Higgins's feelings. Mrs. Baggoli told her to trust her instincts. This time both Jon and Andy got a few lines in before Carla had a question about Henry Higgins's character. I relaxed. This was Carla's big scene. It would take hours.

I drifted off again, thinking about the concert. I had everything more or less worked out. Ella and I had agreed to tell our mothers that we were spending the night with each other. I know a lot about celebrity parties, and they never end till eight in the morning. That meant we could go straight to the station after the party and be back in Dellwood in time for lunch. Simple but foolproof. Getting into the show wasn't a big deal. It would wipe out my personal savings, but I figured I had enough for a ticket from a scalper, the train fare, cabs, and necessary nourishment. But I hadn't done much thinking about clothes, which, as Carla had been pointing out *ad nauseam,* were particularly important. Should I look elegant and sophisticated like the models and movie stars Stu Wolff usually hangs out with? Or should I look natural and unpretentious but unique, so he'd know right away that I was different from other girls? I was still mulling this over when I realized that Mrs. Baggoli was calling me.

"Lola! Lola!"

I looked over. Everyone was staring at me, but the only one who wasn't smiling was Mrs. Baggoli. "Lola!" she repeated. "That was your cue!"

"Maybe you shouldn't put your script away just yet," advised Carla.

14

ONE OF OUR MINOR DETAILS DISAPPEARS

The house was in its usual state of hysterical chaos when I got home. My family may be hopelessly ordinary, but they're not quiet. My mother and my sisters were in the kitchen, screaming at each other. Two of them were crying. None of them paid any attention to me.

I stood in the doorway for a few seconds, thinking of poor, only-child Ella, all alone in her big quiet house with her doting parents listening to her every word. Boo hoo.

My close female relatives suddenly noticed me standing there. Not that it occurred to them to say "hello" or "how are you?" or anything like that. Instead, the three of them immediately began telling me what had happened as quickly and loudly as they could. It was hard to follow—and not worth the trip. As far as I could make out, Pam took something of Paula's and broke it, so Paula hit Pam, so Pam ran crying to my mother, so my mother yelled at Paula, so Paula started crying, and then, while my mother was giving them Lectures 288 and 289: Sharing and Violence, Pam threw an apple at Paula and my mother whacked Pam with the dishtowel.

"Ah, Lola," I shouted into the general din. "How was your day? How did rehearsals go? What will you be wearing on opening night?"

Paula and Pam kept shrieking, but my mother stopped talking and looked at me for less time than it takes a spark to die in a tornado.

"I should think you'd be wearing your costumes on opening night."

I gestured despairingly. "I mean *after*. At the cast party."

"This isn't Broadway," said my mother. "You have a closet full of clothes. Wear whatever you want."

What I wanted was a drop-dead gorgeous dress that would make me look twenty-five and so sophisticated I should have a perfume named after me.

"But everyone's going to be really dressed up," I informed her. "Carla Santini—"

"Please," begged my mother. "Not Carla Santini again. Isn't there anyone else at your school?"

You'd think she actually listened to me now and then.

"It's my big night," I reminded her. "I want to look right."

"Forget it," said my mother. "There's no way you're getting a new dress, Mary. Last week it was the kiln, and this week it's the car. I can't afford it."

"Who asked?" I snapped back. "I didn't ask for

anything. God knows I wouldn't expect anyone in this house to worry about me. To care about how I look on one of the most important nights of my life. I'll just don my usual rags, shall I? Maybe you'd like me to wear a bag over my head as well. That way no one will be able to report you for neglect of a minor."

Paula looked at my mother. "What's Mary talking about?"

My mother rolled her eyes.

Pam looked at me. "Why are you wearing a bag over your head? How are you going to be able to see?"

My mother patted Pam's shoulder. "Don't worry, honey," she said kindly. "Mary can cut eyes in the bag."

"How typical!" I proclaimed. "How typical that you would mock me in my torment."

"What does torment mean?" asked Paula, as I turned on my heels and marched from the room.

"It means Mary's had a bad day," said my mother.

Ella hadn't thought much about what she was wearing.

"I'm trying not to think about it at all," Ella admitted. "I get cold chills every time I do. It makes it seem so real." She shuddered. "I just know something's going to go wrong."

"Nothing's going to go wrong," I assured her. "My plan is awesome in its simplicity."

Ella would ask her mother if she could stay over at

my house; I'd ask my mother if Ella could stay at ours. Mrs. Gerard would call my mother to make sure it was all right. Then, after that was all settled, I'd tell my mother we'd changed our minds and I was going to Ella's instead. My mother would never think of calling Mrs. Gerard to make sure it was all right. She'd just assume that it was.

I flopped down on the couch beside Ella. Mrs. Gerard wasn't there. Mrs. Gerard was taking a course in aromatherapy. She said essential oils helped her to de-stress. I couldn't see that Mrs. Gerard had the kind of life that stressed you out, but, as the great philosophers say, everything is relative.

"Well, you're going to have to think about it. It's not that far away."

"I know," said Ella. "I know." She bent down and took two uncreased magazines from the neat stacks under the coffee table. "I guess the first thing we should do is decide what kind of thing we want to wear."

We spent the afternoon flipping through her mother's magazines. The only magazines my mother subscribes to involve ceramics, but Mrs. Gerard gets every women's glossy going. Reading them one after the other was like being in a hall of mirrors; you know, lots of images of the same thing.

On every page were beautiful models wearing beautiful clothes and stunning accessories. *Shoes: $175, Handbag: $250, Dress: $900 . . .*

I leaned back in frustration. If Mrs. Gerard wanted to know about stress, she should have had my life.

"What's the use?" I cried. "You can get something perfect. Your parents give you money just for breathing, but I can't afford more than a pair of tights." It was galling to think that such a great and noble enterprise should be brought to its knees by a mere dress.

Ella put the magazine I'd abandoned back in its place.

"Well, why don't I lend you some money to buy something?" she suggested. "You can pay me back whenever."

"No." I shook my head firmly. "I appreciate the offer, but I can't accept charity. We Ceps have our pride."

"It isn't charity," reasoned Ella. "It's a loan. Only no time limit and no interest."

I shook my head even more firmly.

"I still can't. I don't like to borrow money." This is my mother's fault. My mother hates debt. "If you can't afford it, don't buy it," my mother always says. She'd rather eat rice and beans for a week than bounce a check at the supermarket. That's why we waited so long to move out of The City; if she hadn't inherited some money from an aunt in Seattle, none of this would ever have happened.

Ella heaved with exasperation. "Well, let me give you some as a present. An early birthday present."

"Thank you," I said. "Really. But I just can't accept." I didn't see that much difference between charity and a birthday present months in advance.

Ella held up her hands and slapped the air. She was becoming a pretty good actor herself.

"All right . . . all right . . . what if I lend you a dress? I've got tons of things."

I didn't know how to say no. I mean, Ella's the best friend I've ever had, the sister of my soul. How do you tell the sister of your soul that you'd rather spend the rest of your life doing toothpaste commercials than wear something of hers? Ella's taste in clothes had been loosening up since I'd known her, but it was still pretty tight.

"That's a great idea." I sounded pleased and excited. "Let's take a look."

Ella likes pastels. Winter, summer, spring, and fall, Ella wears shades, not colors. And white. I tend to avoid white; I like to wear things more than once before I have to wash them. I also like to wear things that move and flow; Ella is more partial to the simple, tailored look favored by businesswomen.

Ella pulled a powder-blue dress from her closet. "What about this one?" She sounded pretty fed up with pulling dresses from her closet.

I cocked my head to one side, pretending to be considering it as carefully as I'd considered all the others. It was a sleeveless A-line with a row of tiny pearls down the front. I'd rather wear one of those old-fashioned black nun's habits. At least they're mysterious and dramatic.

"I don't think so," I said carefully. "It's a little young."

"You're a little young," snapped Ella. She put the dress back, then turned to me with her hands on her hips. "Why don't you just admit it, Lola? You can't stand the way I dress."

"It's not that," I lied. "It's just that this has to be really special. It has to be glamorous and sophisticated. It has to make a statement."

"You mean like Eliza's ball gown," said Ella.

I gazed back at her, slightly stunned. Maybe her dress sense was better than I'd thought.

Eliza's dress for the ball—in our adaptation, a celebrity charity ball—was absolutely perfect. Because most of the women in Deadwood take classes the way other people take vitamins, Mrs. Baggoli doesn't have any trouble finding seamstresses to make the costumes for our plays. Mine had been copied by Mrs. Trudeo from an haute couture design. It was red satin and long and devastatingly simple. As I said, I prefer full, flowing skirts, but even I had to admit this dress was hot. My mother was lending me a pair of red satin stilettos, leftover from the days when Elk used to drag her out dancing.

I spread my arms, already feeling the warmth of hope beginning to run through me.

"Exactly." Even Mrs. Baggoli said it made me look at least twenty. "That's exactly the kind of dress I mean."

"Well, then your problem's solved, isn't it?" said Ella sarcastically. She was still smarting from my rejection of her clothes. "All you have to do is ask Mrs. Baggoli if you can borrow it."

I was so excited at supper that night that it took all of my considerable professional skills to act like the only thing I had on my mind was washing my hair. I forced myself to eat, even though about ten million miniature ballerinas were dancing in my stomach. I forced myself to listen to the two-headed monster's description of the day's thrilling events. I made myself laugh at my mother's jokes. I even made a show of paying attention when she explained the problems she was having with the glaze for her new line of mugs.

But all the while, I was thinking about that ball gown. At least now I knew what I wanted to wear. In a dress like that I would make an entrance; a statement. It didn't even worry me that Carla would see me in the dress. So what? She was going to be so stunned, not just to see me there, but to see the way Stu Wolff reacted to the sight of me, that she wasn't going to know what I was wearing. And Stu Wolff *would* notice me in that dress. He couldn't help but notice me. Notice me? If I turned up dressed like that he'd probably trip over himself trying to get to meet me. I could see him blush shyly; hear him say, "I hope you won't think I'm too pushy, but I'd really like to dance with you."

"Why's Mary smiling like that?" asked Paula, loud

enough to sabotage my elaborate fantasy.

"It must be something I said," said my mother. "Was it about going back to the electric blue, or was it about mixing softener with the slip?"

I made a face at Paula. "I was just smiling, that's all. Is it a crime to smile in this family all of a sudden?"

"Not a crime," said my mother. "But it means you weren't really listening. It could be considered a misdemeanor."

I gave her a mocking smile.

Obviously, I couldn't actually ask Mrs. Baggoli if I could borrow Eliza's dress, if for no other reason then that she'd say no and I would have no recourse. Not only were all the costumes school property, but mine was Mrs. Trudeo's project for Advanced Dessmaking; it had to go back after the last performance to be graded. But I couldn't *not* ask Mrs. Baggoli and just take it home for the weekend, because all the costumes were locked away in the drama club closet for safekeeping. Only Mrs. Baggoli and Mrs. Ludley, the janitor, had keys.

But at least I knew what I was aiming for. I would comb the thrift stores of Deadwood; I would bike to all the nearby towns and comb their thrift stores. I was bound to come up with something. I could feel it in my bones.

"So, Mary, you're all right to do that for me tomorrow?" shouted my mother, rather as if she'd said it before.

"Do what?"

"Pick up the car at the garage. I have to get this order finished by Sunday."

"In the afternoon," I said quickly. "I have something to do in the morning."

That night I dreamed Ella and I were at the concert. We were in the front row, right in the middle. Carla Santini was there, too, of course. She was sitting in the front, but to the side. She was wearing a very expensive and sophisticated dress—black to match her heart—but she might as well have been wearing a blue flannel and a baseball cap with her Calvin Klein jeans as far as Stu Wolff was concerned. He must have walked past Carla at least a hundred times as he danced around the stage, but he never gave her a second look. He noticed me in my red satin dress, my hair down and my eyes dark and passionate, looking like a gypsy queen while he was singing my all-time favorite Sidhartha song, "Only with You." (*Only with you does this world seem all right. . . . Only with you do I see a true light. . . .*) From then on he sang every song right to me. I didn't smile or giggle or do anything silly like Carla would have done. I just sat there, my eyes looking into his, reading his heart and his soul as surely as he read mine. At the end of the last encore, Stu picked up a red rose someone had thrown at him earlier, leaned over the stage, and handed it to me as though it were a precious jewel. I stood on my tiptoes to reach his kiss.

I could still feel his lips on mine when I woke up.

I was outside the first thrift store by ten.

"Describe it to me again?" said Mrs. Magnolia. Mrs. Magnolia ran Second Best, the sixth thrift store I tried.

"It's the kind of dress Scarlett O'Hara might have worn if she wanted to break every heart in Atlanta," I explained for the third time. "But modern. No hoops or anything."

Mrs. Magnolia shook her head, her eyes moving past the racks of sweatshirts and sweaters that took up most of the store.

"I don't think we have anything even close to that," she informed me sadly, "but you're welcome to look in the formal-dress section."

"I have looked." The formal-dress section contained nothing but bridesmaid dresses in the colors of cheap candy. I gave her the hopeful look of a kid on a Christmas card. "I was just wondering if maybe you had stuff in the back. You know, stuff that hasn't been put out yet."

Mrs. Magnolia started shaking her head again. "Oh, yes, yes . . . but it hasn't been sorted and tagged. It's not ready for sale."

"Well, couldn't I just kind of look through it?"

I was beginning to wonder if Mrs. Magnolia was ever going to stop shaking her head.

"Oh, no, no, dear, I'm afraid that's out of the question." She pointed to the door at the back of the room. On it was a hand-written Employees Only sign. "It's against our rules."

"But Mrs. Magnolia," I pleaded, my voice hoarse with despair. "Mrs. Magnolia, I'm desperate. I've been to every thrift store between here and Dellwood." The concert was only a week away. I threw myself across the counter. "I have got to have that dress! It's a matter of life and death!"

"I'm sure there's nothing like you're describing," said Mrs. Magnolia. "This isn't really a Scarlett O'Hara kind of town." But she'd stopped shaking her head: she was weakening.

I straightened up, my face radiant. "What if I do the sorting, Mrs. Magnolia? For nothing."

"Nothing" did the trick.

"Follow me," said Mrs. Magnolia. "I'll show you what to do."

By the time I got home that afternoon I was totally distraught. All those hours! All that pedaling! All that work! And what did I have to show for it? Aching muscles, a clinical dislike of synthetic fabrics, and a depression Hamlet would have recognized. But no dress to wear to the ball. I was Cinderella but without the fairy godmother.

My mother was totally distraught by the time I got home, too. She must have been watching for me from her studio because she was in the driveway by the time I pulled in. She was wearing her work clothes and was covered with clay.

"Where on earth have you been?" my mother demanded. "It's nearly four o'clock. I thought you promised to pick up the car."

I'd forgotten about the car.

My mother didn't wait for my excuse; nor did she take any pity on the fact that I was dirty, sweaty, smelled of old clothes, and was traumatized by disappointment. She turned me right around. If I hurried I could make it before the garage closed.

"Remember!" she shouted after me. "Not Jay's." Jay was our old mechanic, but he'd sold the business to someone else and my mother didn't like the new guy. "The one on Stanley."

I'd never been to the one on Stanley before but had no trouble finding it; it was the only garage on the street. The yard was full of cars in different states of destruction, and there was a Closed sign in the office window. My heart hit the ground like someone thrown out of an airplane. Karen Kapok was going to kill me. Probably slowly.

I was just about to turn around again and ride back into the jaws of death when I realized that all was not lost. The garage itself was still open. There was a pair of combat boots sticking out from under an old Karmann

146

Ghia that was pieced together with parts from so many different cars that it looked like a patchwork quilt on wheels. A portable stereo was blaring. I drove straight into the garage and screeched to a stop by the boots.

"Hi," I said. No answer. I raised my voice. "Hello? Hello?" I shouted above the roar of The Clash. "I'm here to pick up Karen Kapok's car?"

From under the car a male voice finally replied.

"What?"

I bent down closer to the feet.

"I'm here to pick up Karen Kapok's car!" I screamed.

"Lola?"

The feet moved and the body followed.

"Sam?" I should have recognized the boots. Sam Creek is the only boy in Deadwood not in ROTC who wears combat boots. "What are you doing here?"

Sam sat up on the dolly. His dreads were tucked up under a filthy knit hat. If you discounted the ring in his nose, he looked almost normal. "I'm working on my car." He jerked his head. "This is my old man's place."

"Oh, thank God." Ignoring the grease and the grime, I sank down beside him. "I was afraid I was too late. I came to get my mother's car."

"You are too late," said Sam. "The office is locked." He wiped his grease-smeared forehead with his grease-stained sleeve. "And the keys to your mom's car are in the office."

Stricken with despair, I groaned. "Oh no . . . now what am I going to do? My mother's going to murder me." I buried my face in my hands. "Does God hate me, or something?" I looked up and groaned again. "I can't believe you can't get into the office."

Sam gave me the wise-guy smile that has so endeared him to the students and staff of Deadwood High.

"I didn't say I can't get in," said Sam. "I just said it was locked."

I'd never seen anyone unlock a door without a key before. It was pretty impressive.

"Where'd you learn to do that?" I asked.

"Oh, I'm a man of many talents," said Sam, and he slipped inside. He was back in a few seconds with my mother's key chain dangling from his fingers.

I was practically prostrate with gratitude and relief.

"I can't thank you enough," I told Sam. "My mother really would have killed me."

He laughed. "Consider it a token of my appreciation for all you've done to get up Carla Santini's nose since you've been here. It's a joy to watch." He handed me the keys. "Not everyone can take on The Santini and survive."

"I know," I said. "Ella told me what happened to Kali Simpson—that she had to move and everything."

Sam shook his head. "That was really sick, what she did to Kali. And what she did to Ella, too."

I gave him a curious look. "What she did to Ella?" Ella had left that bit out of her account of interesting facts about the history of Deadwood and its princess. "What'd Carla do to Ella?"

It was Sam's turn to look curious. "Ella didn't tell you?" He shrugged. "No, I guess she wouldn't."

According to Sam, it happened just before I moved to Deadwood last spring. Ella was friends with Michael Jasper. Michael Jasper is a year ahead of me, so he isn't in any of my classes, but I know who he is. He's the prince of the BTWs. Michael and Ella were very good friends. They were always hanging around together, in and out of school. Everyone knew they were interested in each other. But only Carla Santini decided to do something about it.

"You mean Carla stopped them from getting together?"

"You know Carla," said Sam. "She can't stand seeing someone having something she thinks she should have, even if she doesn't really want it." He wiped some grease on his forehead with the sleeve of his shirt. "I don't know any of the gory details," he went on, "but Ella kind of froze up. I know she isn't the biggest extrovert in the world, but even I could see the difference. She didn't even seem really mad, just kind of surprised. You know, like her mother had suddenly pulled a gun out over supper and shot her in the heart."

I shook my head, trying to take it all in. "My God . . . they'd been friends since forever."

Sam laughed. "Forever's not that long for Carla

Santini. She swanned around for a couple of weeks, hanging on to Mike like he was a helium balloon, and then she dumped him. But not before she'd totally humiliated Ella. You know, making sure Ella saw her and Mike kissing and crap like that, lording it over Ella every chance she got. It was enough to make you puke." His face had been intensely serious, but now he smiled. "So," said Sam, "if you ever need my help in your war against The Santini, all you have to do is ask."

All you have to do is ask. . . .

I stood there, staring at him. I now had more reason than ever to show up Carla Santini. I *had* to go to the party. I had to have Eliza's dress. Sam Creek could get into the closet.

I smiled. "Well, it's funny you should say that," I said.

15

MY LIFE OF CRIME

We waited till Friday, the day before the concert, to take the dress. Sam said that the best time to liberate Eliza's gown from its prison would probably be during rehearsals. There were too many people around during the day, and if we waited till night, there was the problem of the alarms. While I was in the auditorium, my eyes firmly fixed on Mrs. Baggoli, Sam would slip into the drama club room, open the closet, take out the dress and put it in the trash bag I'd provided, and then wait for me in his car. The following Monday, we'd repeat the procedure in reverse. Mrs. Baggoli wouldn't be in on Monday, so the dress would be back long before anyone realized it had gone.

I didn't say anything to Ella about borrowing the dress. All I said was that I'd found the perfect thing to wear. I decided it would be better to present the liberation as a *fait accompli*. If Ella knew what Sam and I were up to, she'd worry—and if she worried too much, she might change her mind about going.

Crime has never really appealed to me as a way of life. True, you get to do a lot of acting, but it's stressful and repetitive. I was, however, willing to step outside the strict boundaries of the law because this was a good, a just, and a noble cause.

Nonetheless, I was a wreck through the entire rehearsal on Friday. To begin with, Carla did nothing but talk about the concert whenever she could. "Are you as excited as I am?" she kept asking me. "Have you decided what you're going to wear?"

During our first break, she made a big deal of saying, "Don't worry, Lola, I won't forget the camera. I know everyone'll be dying to see the photo of you and me together."

One of the stagehands choked back a laugh. "Are you kidding?" he muttered. "We're making bets."

Besides being wound up like a toy by Carla, I kept thinking I could hear footsteps behind the stage, and doors banging. I forgot my lines; I missed my cues. Carla could only have been more pleased if I'd resigned from the play.

"Why don't we take a five-minute break?" called Mrs. Baggoli. "I'm feeling a little cold. I think I'll get my sweater from the drama club room."

I practically fell off the stage, I jumped so fast.

"I'll get it for you, Mrs. Baggoli," I offered. "You just wait right there. I'll be back in a second."

"That's all right, Lola." Mrs. Baggoli held up her key ring. "It's locked."

Locked! My heart had been moving faster than a zebra with a lion on its tail all afternoon, but now it stopped suddenly. What if Sam couldn't get into the drama club room? What if it took him a while to get it open and he was still inside? I raced from the stage to cut off Mrs. Baggoli in the hall.

"Mrs. Baggoli!" I screamed, charging down the stairs and falling into step beside her. The club room was only a few yards ahead of us. "Mrs. Baggoli, I was wondering if I could ask you a question about that last scene."

Mrs. Baggoli gave me a "not you too" look.

"There's no need to shout, Lola," said Mrs. Baggoli. "You're not on-stage now."

How wrong she was!

I went on as though she'd said "yes."

"It's Henry," I said, sliding in front of her. "I'm not sure I really understand his feelings about Eliza."

"Really?" said Mrs. Baggoli. "I should have thought his feelings were an open book to all of us by now. We've been through them enough times with Carla."

"I mean his deep, inner feelings. His—"

Mrs. Baggoli put a hand on my shoulder. "Lola," she said, "would you please get out of my way so I can get my sweater?"

I threw myself against the door. "I know we've discussed it before superficially—" I began, as I danced backward into the drama club room and almost fell over.

Mrs. Baggoli didn't even ask me if I was all right.

"That's funny," she said, looking puzzled. "I was sure I locked that door."

A great actor has to be able to recover quickly from minor setbacks—like a flubbed line, or not knowing that the door wasn't shut right. I recovered quickly enough to notice a bit of red satin sticking through the crack in the closet door while Mrs. Baggoli was checking that nothing had been taken from the desk. I hurled myself in front of the crack.

"You probably did lock it," I assured her. "We have a lock like that at home. Sometimes it works and sometimes it doesn't."

Mrs. Baggoli shut the bottom desk drawer. "Well, nothing seems to be missing. . . ." She removed her sweater from the back of the chair. "Maybe I didn't lock it after all."

"So, Mrs. Baggoli," I said. "What do you think of Henry's feelings?"

Mrs. Baggoli gave me a look that was very similar to the one my mother always gives me when I confuse her.

"You know, Lola," said Mrs. Baggoli as she shoved me out of the room, "I think maybe you've been working too hard. There's no rehearsal until Tuesday. Why don't you really try to relax this weekend?"

It was raining by the time rehearsal was over. Heedless of the tempest kicking up around me, I streaked across the parking lot to where the multi-colored Karmann Ghia was waiting. The engine started before I reached the door.

"Oh, my God!" I cried as I dropped—more or less literally—into the passenger's seat. "I was really scared for a few minutes there."

"You?" Sam laughed derisively. "I was just about to stuff the dress in the bag when you started shouting in the hall. I felt like I'd been caught by the cops."

I looked around enquiringly. There isn't much room inside a Karmann Ghia. "Where's the dress? In the trunk?"

"The trunk's filled with junk." Sam jerked his head toward the rear. "I put it back there."

I looked behind us. The trash bag had been crammed into the rear seat that had been provided for people who only give rides to very small children.

"Let's get out of here," I ordered, snapping my seat belt. "The sooner I get it home, the happier I'll be."

But instead of putting the car in gear, Sam rolled down his window. I looked over his shoulder. Mrs. Baggoli was running toward us through the downpour. Of course, who else would it be?

"Oh, no . . . ," I moaned softly. We were doomed. No wonder they always say crime doesn't pay.

Sam leaned out the window. "What's the problem, Mrs. Baggoli?" he asked as though there were nothing on the back seat at all.

It's amazing how many people who have no interest in the theater can act.

"It's my car," gasped Mrs. Baggoli. She sounded fraught. "It won't start."

Sam went with Mrs. Baggoli to see what was wrong with her car while I waited in the Karmann Ghia. I kept glancing behind me to make sure the dress was still there—and still in its bag.

After what seemed like hours of agony, Sam came back. He opened my door. Mrs. Baggoli was with him.

"We're giving Mrs. Baggoli a ride home." He gave me a "what could I do" look. "You see if you can squeeze into the back."

"The back?"

"I don't want to put you two to any trouble," Mrs. Baggoli was saying from over his shoulder. "I didn't realize your car was so small. I can call a cab."

I could easily imagine what would happen then. All too well. The storm would increase, the cab wouldn't turn up, Mrs. Baggoli would start walking home as night fell and the first trees were flung to the ground by the gale-force winds. . . . They might not find her body for days. And whose fault would it be? First I steal the dress from under Mrs. Baggoli's nose, and then I kill her.

"Don't be ridiculous, Mrs. Baggoli," I said quickly. "There's plenty of room."

To illustrate this statement, I stretched over the front seat and flung myself on top of the bag.

Mrs. Baggoli peered into the car. "What if I take that bundle on my lap? That would give you more room back there."

Stifling a cry of excruciating pain, I wedged myself in on top of the dress.

"No, no, it's fine." I tried to make a little room for my left hip. "It's actually surprisingly comfortable."

Sam got in behind the wheel. "So, Mrs. Baggoli, where do you live?"

16

ONCE MORE INTO THE BREACH

The night before the concert was a restless one for me. Killer wasps buzzed in my stomach. Wild stallions stampeded through my heart. Stu Wolff, I repeated over and over to myself, by this time tomorrow you'll be dancing with Stu Wolff. . . . Or talking to him. Or laughing with him. Or just gazing into his eyes with cosmic love. . . .

Minutes passed like hours; hours dragged by like days. There were moments in that dark torment when I thought the sun would never rise again. But the day of the concert finally dawned.

It was a moody morning, gray and cold and mildly vicious. I didn't care about the weather, of course. I was going to meet Stu Wolff. I was going to dance in his arms. A blizzard couldn't have stopped me now. I'd find snowshoes. I'd find a team of dogs and a sled. One way or another, I'd get to Manhattan.

Too excited to go through the motions of daily life— eating and talking to my family—I stayed in my room until Ella arrived, shortly after three. There was a four o'clock train that would get us to The City by six. That gave us two hours to find tickets and wait with the bereaved but adoring multitudes for the concert to begin.

Ella was edgy and a little wild-eyed, like the heroine in a romantic novel. I made a mental note that this was a look she should be encouraged to maintain. It made her look less bland.

"This is the most exciting thing I've ever done," Ella gasped as she shut the door of my room behind her. "But it's also the most terrifying."

I looked her up and down. She had a black bag with her pajamas and toothbrush in it, but nothing else.

"Where's your stuff?" I was afraid that, in her agitated state, she'd forgotten her clothes for the party.

Ella flung herself on the bed.

"I left my bag outside, under that big bush. I didn't want your mother to see it." I was touched by her thoroughness. Maybe she was going to be better at this than I'd feared.

"What about your mom?" I asked. "Do you think you convinced her not to call?"

"I think so," said Ella. "Anyway, she hasn't been nagging me so much lately; she's been kind of distracted. And she has some charity thing to go to tonight. That'll keep her occupied."

Beginning to relax a little, Ella scanned the room.

"So," she said. "Where's your dress?"

"I'll show it to you later," I promised. Now wasn't the time to make her more nervous; I could do that when it was too late to turn back.

"Show it to me now," insisted Ella. "We have time."

I picked up my bag and slipped the strap over my shoulder. "I'm too anxious. Let's tell my mom we're going to your house after all, and get to the station. I'll show you there."

"You can't be as anxious as I am," said Ella. "Every time my mom spoke to me last night and this morning I practically jumped out of my skin." She stood up. "And I couldn't sleep." As though this was enough justification for boldness, Ella grabbed hold of the front flap on my bag. "Come on," she urged. "Just one little pee—"

Ella's mouth held the shape of the word "peek" for several seconds, but no sound came out. Her eyes met mine.

"I don't believe it." She was calm like a dead sea. "I don't believe you *stole* Eliza's gown!"

Language is a subtle and intricate thing.

"I didn't steal it. I borrowed it."

Ella pounced. "You borrowed it? You mean you asked Mrs. Baggoli and she said it was okay?"

I gestured vaguely. "Well, no . . . not exactly. . . ."

"Exactly what, then?" asked Ella. "I thought Mrs. Baggoli kept the costumes locked up."

I nodded, glad to be able to give a positive response. "Yeah, she does. But Sam Creek—"

"Sam Creek?" Ella looked as though there would be no more surprises for her in life; she'd seen it all. "You mean you got Sam involved in this? *He* stole the dress for you?"

"Borrowed," I corrected. "Sam borrowed it for me. Calm down, will you? It'll be back in the closet by Monday afternoon, and no one will be the wiser." I shut the bag. "And besides," I concluded, "technically, it is *my* dress."

"No it isn't," said Ella. "*Technically,* it's Mrs. Trudeo's. She's the one who made it."

"For *me,*" I countered. "She made it for me." For me and Advanced Dressmaking, Spring Term.

Ella collapsed back on the bed. "Lola, I can't go through with this," she announced. "It's bad enough that I'm lying to my parents, but stolen goods is something else. You're never going to get away with it."

I grabbed her arm and pulled her to her feet. "You can't back out now," I said. "You just can't."

Ella's cry was tinged with despair. "Oh, Lola . . ."

As many people are in life, Ella was torn between the need for excitement and the demands of terror. She wanted to go to the concert and the party; but she didn't want to go to jail. I could understand that. I didn't want to go to jail, either.

"Ella, please . . . the deed's done. If I am going to get caught, at least let me wear the dress. At least let me have one night of pure joy if I'm going to spend the rest of my precious youth behind bars."

Ella didn't say "yes," but she didn't say "no," either.

I pushed my advantage.

"And besides," I went on, "unless you turn me in, you're already an accessory after the fact."

I had no idea what "an accessory after the fact" was. It's something they say in cop shows. But, like Mr. Santini, Ella's father is a lawyer. She seemed to know what it meant.

"This better be one great party," said Ella.

"Stop!" shrieked Ella. "I think I've cracked a rib."

At the time, I was trying to find a position that would let me move enough to pull off my jeans. "Oh, don't be so melodramatic," I said. "You couldn't have cracked a rib. There's not enough room in here."

Neither Ella (who, admittedly, had led a very sheltered life) nor I (who at least once resided in a metropolis teeming with life on all levels) had ever actually tried to dress in the restroom of a train before. If we had, we definitely wouldn't have tried it again.

"But I'm in pain," wailed Ella. "Can't you move back just a little?"

I glared at her, though she probably didn't notice because the lighting was so bad.

"Maybe we should take turns then," said Ella.

I shook my head, and banged it against the flimsy wall. "No. We need each other to zip up and put on our makeup." I fell onto the toilet as the train took a sudden bend. "And, anyway, we're already half undressed. We may as well keep going."

We kept going, but, unfortunately, the train kept

going, too. My memory of the route to The City was that it was pretty straight, but either my memory was wrong or the route had been changed to take in every bend between Dellwood and New York. It was lucky the restroom was no bigger than a broom closet or Ella and I would have spent a lot of time on the floor.

Bruised and exhausted, we finally got our regular clothes off and our party dresses on.

"What do you think?" asked Ella.

"It's a little hard to tell when we're practically touching noses." I wedged my makeup bag behind the sink. "Let's do our faces, and then we can check ourselves outside."

As I always say, you live and you learn. Changing in a moving train turned out to be nothing next to putting on makeup in a moving train. Putting on makeup in a train that's speeding through the sleepy suburbs is like trying to eat a bowl of hot soup on a roller coaster. And no less painful. If I wasn't poking myself in the eye with my liner, I was poking my elbow in Ella. And it was no more successful than eating soup on a roller coaster either. In the end, we took turns bracing ourselves against the door while the other one very carefully applied the mascara and the blush.

"That's going to have to do," said Ella. She pulled back as far as she could to examine her handiwork. "I'm afraid I'm going to blind you."

"Do I look sophisticated and enigmatic?"

Ella cocked her head to one side. "Yeah," she said slowly. "You do. Of course, you also look like you've been crying a lot." Mascara can really sting.

"It'll clear," I said dismissively.

"And the eyeliner's not totally even."

"I can live with it for now. I'll fix it when we're on *terra firma*. Let's just get out of here before we suffocate."

Once we got out of the restroom, we took a long critical look at each other.

"You look fantastic," said Ella. "Even though your eyes are still bloodshot." She nervously licked her lips. "What about me?"

It had been a Herculean task, but after months of trying, I'd finally managed to talk Ella into wearing her hair down. But besides convincing her to throw away her hair tie, I'd also convinced her to buy something for the party that wasn't so basic you could wear it to church in the morning and a cocktail party in the evening: a full black taffeta skirt and a black lace body-suit. The transformation was astounding. Henry Higgins couldn't have been half as pleased with Eliza as I was with Ella. In her regular clothes and with her hair up, Ella looked like she was practicing for middle age; in the black ensemble with her hair down, she looked like the mysterious heroine from a gothic novel.

"You look spectacular," I assured her. "Eat your heart out, Carla Santini. Your day of reckoning has come at last!"

Ella and I found two seats facing backward, so that we watched New Jersey disappear rather than New York City approach.

"I can't believe this!" Ella kept saying. She was practically vibrating with excitement. "We're really doing it. We're really going to see Sidhartha!" She squeezed my arm. "Lola, we're really going to see Sidhartha!" She was smiling so much that even though it had started to rain, it seemed like a sunny day. "Me! I've never even been on a train before without my mother."

Inside, my heart and soul were in ecstatic turmoil, but on the outside I was trying to be cool. All of the other passengers were dressed as you would expect people to be dressed on a Saturday afternoon: you know, normal. Ella and I were attracting a lot of attention. I don't usually mind attracting attention, but I was worried that one of the anonymous women with her bag on her lap and a paperback in her hands might be a friend or acquaintance of Mrs. Gerard who would recognize Ella and want to know what she was doing on a train without parental supervision.

"Keep it down, will you?" I hissed. "The whole car can hear you."

But it was too late for caution.

The woman behind us leaned over the seat and tapped me on the shoulder.

As soon as I felt her hand on me, I started thinking of excuses: my mother was in the next car; we were going to a masquerade party; Ella who?

"Excuse me," she said, "but where are the cameras?"

Ella groaned. "Oh, my God, Lola. We didn't bring a camera!"

"Oh, I'm so sorry." The woman laughed. "It's the clothes. . . ." She laughed again. "I thought you must be shooting a commercial."

A commercial! Me and Ella! Carla Santini was going to die.

17

THE BEST LAID PLANS OF MICE AND MEN
OFTEN GET MESSED UP

I had no trouble imagining Carla Santini's arrival in New York City. Except for the lack of ticker tape and cheering crowds, she glided into the metropolis like visiting royalty, watching the teeming multitudes from behind the tinted windows of her father's Mercedes while she thought about how awful it must be not to be her. The pearl-gray sedan silently slid to a stop behind the Garden. A uniformed doorman opened a solid-steel door, and Carla Santini stepped out into the rainy evening, cool and relaxed, her dress unwrinkled, her makeup flawless, her press pass in her hand. The doorman held an umbrella over her head as he led her inside, lest one small drop should mar her perfection. "Miss Santini," he cooed. "Please step this way."

At about the same time that I imagined Carla Santini, all teeth and curls, was being offered refreshment in the Garden's VIP lounge, Ella and I made our own, less auspicious arrival in New York.

"I'm sure I read somewhere that Stu Wolff's a very

regular, down-to-earth guy," Ella was saying as we fought our way out of Penn Station. "His dad's a truck driver or something like that, and he loves baseball and beer. He doesn't like all the show-business hype. He's a real man of the people."

I grabbed her arm and pulled her past a few of "the people"—the ones who didn't dress as well as Stu Wolff and who were begging for money.

I didn't want to talk about Stu or what was going to happen anymore. We were there, in my favorite place on the planet, about to meet one of the greatest— and sexiest—poets who'd ever lived. I wanted action, not words.

We hurled ourselves through a herd of travelers trying to get into the building, and then ground to an abrupt halt. It was raining a lot harder in New York than it was in New Jersey.

I let out a heartfelt moan. "Oh, no. We're going to get soaked."

If the storm kept up, we'd look like bag ladies by the time we got downtown. And Eliza's gown would be ruined. For the first time, I realized what incredible potential for disaster our project had. Mrs. Baggoli would kill me if anything happened to the dress. And after she killed me, my mother would probably burn my remains in her kiln.

"It's karma," said Ella. She might have looked like a Pre-Raphaelite model, but she was still her mother's daughter. "You should never have borrowed the dress."

By now even I knew that I shouldn't have borrowed the dress. "Thanks," I muttered.

Ella linked her arm in mine. "Come on," she said with her usual cheerfulness. "We're here now. Let's enjoy ourselves."

I looked at the unmoving traffic and the steady stream of pedestrians and the blur of lights in the downpour. I heard the horns and the shouts and the sirens weaving through the cauldron of sound. I smelled the pretzels and hot dogs and stale urine of the streets. I breathed deeply. New York City! I was back where I belonged. My fear evaporated. The blood began to surge through my veins with its old passion and excitement. Like an eagle, my heart began to soar.

"You're right," I said. "We're young, we're beautiful, we're talented, and we're in the greatest city in the world." I'd been so preoccupied with worrying about the dress that I'd taken the wrong exit and we'd come out across the street from the Garden. I turned us around. "We're going to have an incredible time!" I announced to the general throng. "An absolutely incredible time!"

The light changed. We stepped off the curb together. Ella kept going, but one of my mother's killer heels wedged itself in a sewer grate. My body went forward, but my foot stayed where it was.

I screamed.

The man behind us cursed as he more or less flew over me.

After he'd picked himself off the street, he helped me up.

"If you're going to have such an incredible time," he said, "you better try a little harder to live to enjoy it."

There were about a million kids milling around outside Madison Square Garden, and about half a million cops.

"Geez . . . ," Ella whistled. "I don't think I've ever seen so many people in one place before."

"Come on." I held her tightly. The last thing I needed was to lose Ella. "Let's find someone who's selling tickets."

Ella glanced uneasily at the noisy crowd. "You mean there isn't a stall or something?"

Sometimes I don't think Ella is merely sheltered. Sometimes I think it's more like she's been in solitary for sixteen years.

"No, there isn't a stall."

It took us about fifteen minutes to find a guy with two decent tickets. Because we looked like such nice kids, he was willing to give us a bargain price.

"But that's nearly fifty percent more than they should cost!" Ella blurted out.

Under my tutelage, she was definitely beginning to get over her shyness.

Our benefactor gave her a crooked smile in which teeth were only a memory. "Honey, this gig was sold out before the tickets were printed. You're lucky I'm not asking double."

"But that's—" began Ella.

I kicked her in the ankle.

"We'll take them," I said. It left us with just enough for incidentals, but that didn't matter. It was going to be worth it. We might not even need a cab in the morning. Stu might take us to the station in his Porsche.

I pulled out my wallet. I opened it. All it contained was a five-dollar bill.

The tickets fluttered out of my reach.

"That's not enough," said the ticket seller.

"Don't worry," I assured him. "We have it." I pulled my backpack from my shoulder. Just in case someone tried to mug us, Ella and I had put most of our money in an empty film canister in my makeup bag. I mean, even in New York no one's going to steal your makeup, are they? I stuck my hand in. Or are they?

"What's wrong?" asked Ella.

"Nothing." I squatted on the ground with the bag and started pulling things out. My Converse, my socks, my black jeans, my black turtleneck . . .

"Ella," I wailed. "Ella, it's not here. My makeup bag's not here."

"It must be," said Ella. She bent down beside me. "When do you remember having it last?"

"In the train. Don't you remember? I put it behind the—"

I looked at Ella.

Ella looked at me.

"Sink," finished Ella.

A great actor has to learn to take disappointment and rejection in stride. There will always be the big flop, the bad review, the canceled series. A great actor has to be able to pick herself up, dust herself off, and start all over again.

I am going to be a great actor. Not having a ticket wasn't going to stand in my way.

"This isn't going to work," Ella hissed in my ear.

I tightened my grip on her hand as we finally started shuffling toward the entrance.

"Yes, it will," I hissed back.

It was the old "if you want to hide a tree, put it in a forest" trick. I saw it in a movie. The hero was being chased by the bad guys, and the only chance he had of losing them was to disappear into a packed football stadium. Only he didn't have a ticket. And because he'd had to leave the house in a hurry and had forgotten to take his wallet, he didn't have any money either. So he attached himself to a group of guys from out of town and just strolled right in with them.

The problem was finding a large group of very noisy and active people among whom we could lose ourselves. Most of the kids filing into the concert were in couples. And they had no choice but to be pretty orderly because there were guards on either side of each doorway, taking the tickets one by one.

"It's a little tricky," I admitted, *sotto voce*, "but I think it's possible. Just follow my lead."

Ella started deep breathing. "I'm not going to be able to do this, Lola. I'm terrified."

"Stage fright," I assured her. "It'll pass."

More or less directly in front of us was a group of four handing over their tickets on one side, and a group of five on the other. Between us were two couples. It was now or never. I squeezed Ella's hand.

"Come on," I ordered. "Do what I do."

I edged through the couples in front of us and attached myself to the group of four on the left. Smiling, I started talking to the back of the girl nearest me.

"I'm so excited," I told her, inching forward. "I feel like I've been waiting for this forever. . . . What song do you think they'll start with?" Inch . . . inch . . . "I hope they do 'Love Loser.' That's got to be my all-time favorite. . . . " Inch . . . inch . . . "I wish they let you bring cameras in here. . . . " Inch . . . inch . . . "Wouldn't you just die for a photograph of Stu on-stage?"

Still talking, I stepped into the foyer. My heart was racing; my cheeks were flushed. A hand fell on my shoulder and yanked me backward, none too gently.

"Just a minute," said the young man in the Sidhartha T-shirt, with the radio clipped to his belt. "Let me take another look at your ticket."

I don't know where he came from. He must have

been lying in wait because he wasn't one of the guys at the door.

"My ticket?" I smiled as though I had nothing to hide. "Sure."

I dug my hands into the pockets of my cape, but—to my horror—my ticket wasn't there.

I smiled again. Nervously. "I must have stuck it in my bag," I mumbled. I opened my bag and started shoving things around.

The young man didn't smile back. He just stood there looking both expectant and bored.

"It's not here." My voice was surprised, innocent, confused. I looked at the ground in desperation. "I must have dropped it."

He grabbed hold of my elbow. "Come on," he said. "No ticket, no concert."

"But I have a ticket!" I shouted indignantly. "I had it just a second ago. I—"

"No ticket, no concert," he repeated, dragging me behind him.

I dug in my heels as much as you can on a solid floor. "You can't do this!" In my red satin dress and black velvet cape, I was in one of my *Gone With the Wind* moods. And, like Scarlett O'Hara, I was not about to be trifled with. I tilted my head back defiantly. "I demand to see your supervisor!"

"You can see him outside," he said, and yanked me through the throng moving in the opposite direction and back to where I'd started.

174

"You really want to see the supervisor?" He held on to my elbow. He must have done this before; he wasn't taking any chances.

But I wasn't paying any attention to him by then. I was looking the other way, my eyes on Ella, who was standing on the other side of the entrance, staring at me with a look of shock on her face.

18

THE NIGHT CONTINUES AS IT BEGAN

After we were firmly escorted from the Garden (I re-creating Joan of Arc being led to the stake, the noble head held high; Ella staring at the ground in case someone she knew passed by), we hung around outside with the thousands of other wet, ticketless fans who were mobbing the street. Even if there hadn't been so much noise, we wouldn't have been able to hear what was going on inside, but we could sometimes hear snatches of shouting and conversation and the occasional drum roll or guitar riff. I didn't care. I was as happy as a person who is missing the last performance of a legend could be. I might not have been able to see or hear them, but I was standing on roughly the same piece of ground as Sidhartha; I was breathing the same toxic air. The same rain that poured down on me would pour down on them as they ran to and from their limousines. Once someone must have opened an inside door, because I was sure I head Stu's voice, his actual, warm, rich, unrecorded voice, break into the night like a flame to heat our souls. "What the hell is that supposed to be?" it said.

Even though she wasn't the one who got caught, Ella was still shaken by our close encounter with the law. She stood beside me, shivering slightly, the only island of silence in the sea of shouting fans.

"You know," I said, trying to cheer her up, "you're not such a bad actor yourself."

Instead of panicking when she saw me with the guard, Ella had faked outrage and marched to my defense. "We're together," she'd called out. "What seems to be the problem?" She was so convincing that he didn't even think to ask to see her ticket. But not convincing enough, unfortunately.

"You almost had me believing I had lost my ticket," I praised her.

Ella jammed her hands into her coat pockets. "I was so scared, I think I almost convinced myself." And then she kind of froze the way someone in a horror movie does when an axe suddenly smashes through the front door. "Oh, my God, Lola . . . It never even occurred to me. . . . What if they'd arrested us?" Her expression of terror deepened as the axe shattered the door a second time. "Oh, my God, Lola . . . What would my mother say if I was taken home in a police car?"

She probably wouldn't say anything; she'd just die from the shame.

"It doesn't matter. All that matters is that you aren't being taken home in a police car." Not yet anyway.

Ella, however, wasn't really in a state for the cool balm of logic and reason. The thought of pulling up to

58 Birch Hollow Drive in the back of a police car with the blue light flashing while the neighbors all gawked through their blinds and her father tried to revive her mother was too much for her.

"Maybe we should just go home now," Ella said—again. "Before anything else happens."

"Before anything else happens?" I waved my arms. "Ella, nothing's happened yet."

"Yes, it has," said Ella stubbornly. "We're soaked, you almost broke your neck, we lost all our money, we were almost arrested, and now we're standing in the rain outside the concert. I call that something."

I readjusted my hood, though it was so wet by then that there wasn't really much point. "You can't make an omelette without cracking a few eggs," I said philosophically.

Ella smiled thinly.

I changed my approach.

"Oh, please," I begged, grabbing her hands. "We're so close, El. Stu Wolff's only a few yards away from us. The concert'll be over soon, and then he'll be in the same room with us. We can't give up now. Where would we all be today if Columbus had given up and gone back to Spain? If Paul Revere had decided to stay in bed instead of warning everyone that the British were coming? If the Wright brothers had decided to stick to bicycles?"

Ella looked like she was about to answer me, but I didn't give her a chance.

"Nowhere!" I proclaimed. "That's where we'd be.

There'd be no America. There'd be no satellites. No television. No microwaves or mobile phones. No mesquite chips." Ella loves mesquite chips. "We'd be sitting in mud huts in Europe, eating weeds—that's where we'd be." And anyway, we were in so much trouble already that we might as well go on.

Ella looked thoughtful. She's a great believer in sticking things through.

"I didn't say we should give up . . . ," she murmured.

She was weakening. I moved in, stealthy as a panther.

"Don't you want to see the look on Carla's face when we turn up at the party? Don't you want to see her stop smiling when she sees us talking to Stu? Don't you want to see what happens when everyone finds out that we went, and Carla looks like the fool for a change?"

Ella nodded. "Yeah," she said. "I do."

"Great." I slipped my arm through hers. "It that case, it's time we went downtown."

According to Carla's invitation, which I'd had such foresight to commit to memory, the party was in Soho. Where else? Soho is New York's artistic soul (and therefore America's), and Sidhartha was its voice. Besides, everyone knows that Stu Wolff lives in Soho.

Our plan was to be outside Stu's building when the guests started arriving so we could choose our moment to meld in with the crowd. I figured it would take us at least an hour to get down there on the bus and then find the address, especially with the rain. If we left before the concert actually ended, we'd have plenty of time to reach Soho before everyone else, and even be able to go to a coffee shop to dry off and repair what damage we could.

"Can't you read?" The bus driver pointed to the sign. "Exact change or tokens only."

I felt myself blush. I'd been in the wilderness of Deadwood for less than a year by then, and already I'd forgotten how to ride a city bus. It's my father's fault; whenever I visit him, he insists on walking everywhere.

Ella started digging through her pockets, but I kept my eyes on the five-dollar bill in my hand.

"Please," I pleaded, the shadow of tears in my eyes and voice. "It's my sister." I raised my voice. "She broke her foot, but she can't go to the hospital to have it set until we get there to mind the babies."

"I have a dollar forty in coins," said Ella, dropping several of them on the stairs. "How much do you have?"

I knew how much change I had without looking: fifty-eight cents.

"It's not enough," I said in a voice thick with sadness. Ella started picking up the change she'd dropped. I turned my unhappy eyes on the driver. "Please . . . She had to crawl to the phone to call us. She—"

"Take a cab," said the driver. "It's quicker."

"But we don't have enough for a cab."

There was a shriek of disgust behind me.

180

"Oh, my God!" screamed Ella. "I just saw a cockroach."

No one paid any attention to her. A cockroach on a city bus isn't exactly news.

I waved the bill at the driver. "Don't you understand?" I was practically sobbing. "My poor sister's all alone with three little babies and a broken foot, maybe even a compound fracture. . . . She's lying there in pain, waiting for us to come and save her."

Ella straightened up. "I almost touched it," she squealed. "I almost touched it with my hand."

This statement didn't catch anyone's attention either.

"Look," said the driver. "This isn't an ambulance. It's a city bus. You have to have the exact fare."

Bitter tears of frustration welled in my eyes. "But the littlest is only two months old," I wailed. "Two months old, sir. Do you have children? Do you remember when they were two months old? How they'd lie in their little cribs crying and crying until their mother picked them up and took them in her arms?"

"Look," said the driver, sighing heavily. "It isn't my bus. I just drive it—"

"You do remember!" I was nearly sobbing. "You do know what it's like."

He looked over his shoulder. "Anybody got change for a five?" he called.

19

ON THE STREET WHERE HE LIVES

Ella, shaken from the attack of the killer cockroach, spent the entire ride downtown standing up, watching her feet to make sure nothing with more than two legs walked over them. When she wasn't staring at her shoes, she was darting anxious glances at our fellow travelers. Ella had never been on public transport in New York before. When her parents brought her in they traveled everywhere in cabs. The Gerards don't take any chances.

"Do you think that man back there is crazy?" she whispered.

Pretending that I was reading an advertisement for a computer course, I looked toward the back.

"Which one?" I asked, my eyes now on the headline of the paper the woman sitting in front of us was reading. "The one who's talking to himself, or the one holding up the snake so it can look out the window?"

"Neither," said Ella. "The one wearing the sombrero."

We got off at Fourteenth Street. I knew my way from Fourteenth Street. At least, in dry weather and daylight I did.

"Aren't we there yet?" grumbled Ella.

I got us to Soho okay, but I was having a little trouble finding the exact street we wanted. It was one of those little ones tucked behind a lot of other little streets with funny names. I'm better on the numbered streets and avenues.

Ella stopped and leaned gingerly against a building. She didn't trust touching anything. "My feet are killing me," she moaned.

"Maybe you should put your sneakers back on till we get there," I suggested. Her heels weren't as high as my mother's but they were still significant.

Ella, however, wasn't listening to me. She was looking around us as though she'd just landed on a planet with sixteen moons where everyone lived in glass bubbles and looked like trombones.

"Now what?" I asked.

It was pretty late and the streets were more or less deserted. The only people out were the kind your mother warns you never to talk to, huddled in doorways. It kind of reminded me of old photographs of war-torn Europe.

Ella finally turned back to me with a worried look on her face.

"Are you sure you know where we are?"

"Of course I know where we are," I said with more confidence than I felt. Since I'm being totally honest, I have to admit that I wasn't as knowledgeable about Soho as I could have been. I'd never actually been that far downtown at night by myself. Everything looked different with the shadows and the rain. But I didn't tell Ella that. She was nervous enough.

"This is my city," I assured her. "I know it as well as I know my own room."

Ella gazed at the sodden avenue. "Your room isn't this big," she said, but she sounded relieved.

I pointed to the corner. "I think we go left down there."

We went left, and then we went right, and then we went right, and then we went left, and then we doubled back and went right.

"Why aren't there any policemen around to ask?" Ella complained as we staggered back again to where we'd started.

I was about to repeat my father's joke about New York cops spending all their time in diners eating doughnuts and drinking coffee, but at that instant the gods blew the clouds of hopelessness away.

"Look!" I shouted. "Look what's there!"

Ella looked to where I was pointing. "It's a car stopped at the light."

"No, it's not," I said, already yanking her forward. "It's Mr. Santini's car stopped at the light."

Keeping close to the buildings, and counting on the fact that Carla and Alma, who were sitting together in the back seat, would be looking in the mirror, touching up their makeup, and that Carla's parents, if they did see us, wouldn't recognize us in our new personae as flood victims, Ella and I started to run in the direction of the car.

We caught up with it at the next corner. It turned right. Ella and I went with it. Mr. Santini obviously didn't know Soho any better than I did, because he was going really slow, his eyes on the street signs. We managed to keep up until he shot suddenly to the left down what looked like an alley. I gave a quick look both ways, just as Karen Kapok taught me to, then splashed into the road with Ella in tow.

We raced around the corner; just in time to see the Mercedes turn into the cross street.

"Come on," I said, dragging her on. "He's looking for the address. We must be pretty close."

Ella flapped her arms in a gesture of despair. "So near and yet so far. . . ."

"So near and yet so near," I corrected.

We reached the end of the narrow road and peered cautiously around the corner building.

I squeezed Ella's hand. "I told you!" I hissed. If by some cruel twist of fate I don't become a great actor, I can always become a great detective instead.

Mr. Santini had stopped at the curb in the middle of the next street. We were just in time to see Carla and Alma step out of the plush cocoon of the back seat and into the stormy night, an enormous silver umbrella held high. Carla was dressed to kill (or dressed to roast a turkey) in a short, tight dress—silver to match the umbrella—and silver stilettos. I glanced at my sodden clothes and muddy feet. I looked like someone had tried to kill me. With the umbrella quivering above them like a halo, Carla and Alma glided toward the black door with 63 painted on it in gold.

Mr. Santini leaned across the passenger seat and said something. Ella and I ducked back. When we peeked out again, the Mercedes was pulling away, and Carla was showing her invitation to a very large man in black leather. He looked like the guy you'd find guarding the gates of hell.

"So all we have to do now is get past him," whispered Ella.

"Don't worry," I said. "We've gotten this far. From now on it's a piece of cake."

Ella gave me one of her looks. "Yeah," she muttered. "Fruitcake."

"Plan B isn't going to work," said Ella with new-found authority.

"You mean, unlike Plan A?" I asked sarcastically.

Plan A was Ella's. Plan A entailed sitting in the doorway across from 63 to wait for our chance to crash the party. We'd pushed a few empty beer cans out of our way and sat. And waited. I guess we thought the guests would arrive more or less all at once, like they do for the Oscars and movie premieres, but we were wrong. The guests arrived in dribs and drabs. A car would pull up, a couple of people would jump out and rush to the black door, and the car would vanish back into the night as its passengers vanished inside. Maybe if Stu Wolff's friends really had been just regular guys, we would have been able to sneak in with them, but though he was a man of the people, most of those people drove Jaguars and Porsches, and none of them shopped at K-Mart. There was no way we were going to be able to slip in without at least a dozen of them as camouflage.

"And anyway," I continued, "it is going to work. It's perfect."

I was tired of waiting for a stretch limo with fifteen passengers who'd just been in a boating accident to turn up. I gazed at the black door, shining in the rain, then raised my eyes to the lighted windows of the loft above it. I could see people talking and drinking and having a good time. Music and laughter seeped into the quiet street. I didn't want to sit in the deluge. I wanted to be inside with all the famous people, talking and laughing and dancing the night away. All the women we'd seen enter the building were stunningly beautiful and wearing stunningly beautiful clothes. Stu Wolff would never notice Carla among them. She'd look ordinary in that crowd. But not Ella and me. Stu might think we were homeless runaways, but he'd notice us for sure.

I grabbed Ella's arm. "Don't argue," I ordered. "Let's do it now, before anyone else arrives." I tugged her to her feet. "Plan B, here we come."

Plan B was simple. I'd pretend to be ill, and Ella would ask to use the phone to call my mother to pick us up.

Ella rang the bell. She did it so gently, you'd think she was hoping there was no one home.

"Harder," I whispered. "You want to sound urgent."

She rang it again.

"Ding dong, ding dong," I mimicked. "What are you, the Avon Lady?" I'd been putting myself into the part of someone in intense and unbearable pain, but now I rallied. "Let me do it." I pushed her aside.

"I thought you were supposed to be dying." She pushed me back.

"I'll start dying again after he opens up." I put my finger on the bell and kept it there.

"Stop upstaging me," said Ella, trying to pry my finger off the black button. We were so engrossed in how to ring the bell and who should ring it that we didn't hear anyone coming down the stairs.

The door swung open so suddenly that we almost fell in. That is, we would have fallen in if our way hadn't been blocked by six feet of leather and a face like a wall. The doorman looked a lot bigger up close, and not nearly as charming.

He didn't say anything; he just stood there staring at us in a sullen and inhospitable way.

I groaned and clung to Ella, holding her tightly.

"I—I—I'm sorry to bother you," Ella stammered, "but I was wondering if we could—"

"There's a party going on," he informed us shortly. He had the soft, polite, reasonable voice of a serial killer. "Invitation only."

"Please," I gasped. "We just want to use the phone."

No flicker of compassion showed in those steel-blue eyes.

"This is a private residence, not Grand Central Station. Use a public phone."

"But we have no money," cried Ella. "And my friend's very ill."

Mr. Charm put his hand in his pocket and pulled out some change. "Here," he said. "My treat."

I groaned. "I think I'm going to be sick," I whispered. "Quick! I'm going to be sick."

A slight look of doubt appeared in the granite of his eyes.

"You can't leave us out here!" Ella half commanded, half begged. "My friend's going to throw up on the street."

He hesitated for a second, obviously weakening. "Look, I don't know. . . . I'm really not supposed to let anybody in. . . ." He glanced behind him, as though the answer to his problem might be coming down the stairs.

Ella and I looked, too. Something was coming down the stairs. We could hear a lot of angry shouting and the pounding of hurrying feet. The only words I could make out were ones I can't repeat. All three of us moved to one side as two men came charging down the staircase. Neither of them seemed too steady on his feet.

"Come back here, you idiot!" screamed the one who was behind. Ella gave me a nudge. It was Steve Maya, Sidhartha's lead guitarist. "You can't leave like this. You're making a fool of yourself again."

The man in the lead didn't slow down.

"Don't tell me what I can and can't do!" he screamed back. "It's all over, remember? I'll do what I want!"

"Haven't you always?" screamed Steve Maya. And then, seeing the three of us gawking up at him, he started yelling at the doorman. "Grab him, Mick! Don't let him out!"

The man being pursued stopped at the bottom of the stairs, pointing at the doorman. "You touch me, and your wife's a widow!" he roared.

Mick wasn't sure who to take his orders from. He'd moved to block the door, but now he hesitated, frozen with indecision. Ella and I didn't so much as breathe. We couldn't. We were frozen with awe. All three of us kind of leaned backward as Stu Wolff thundered past us and hurled himself into the stormy night.

Ella looked at me. "Now what?" she whispered.

Life is full of ironies, isn't it? Ella and I had been desperately trying to get into the party, and now the gods had made it possible for us to do just that. Steve Maya had reached the door, and he and Mick were standing there, discussing what they should do next. Paying no attention at all to Ella and me. All we had to do was walk up the stairs and we were in. But the main reason we wanted to be inside was now outside, staggering down the street in the wind.

"Maybe one of us should go after him," Mick was saying. "He could hurt himself."

"I don't care if he hangs himself," said the man who, according to the magazines, has been Stu Wolff's best friend since elementary school.

"Okay," said Mick. "Then he could hurt somebody else. Remember what happened in L.A."

Steve Maya laughed unhappily. "I remember. And I remember Chicago, Frisco, Albany, Tokyo, London, and Manchester, too. . . ." He laughed again. "There's hardly a city in the world where something hasn't happened because of *him*."

I took hold of Ella.

"You know," I said loudly, "I think I'm feeling better. I don't think we have to call my mom after all."

I gave Ella a squeeze.

"Well," she said, picking up her cue. "I guess we'll be going now. My friend's okay."

I nodded. "Yeah, we'll be going now."

We could have saved our breath. Neither of them acted as though we'd spoken.

Mick's eyes were still on the street. "You sure you don't want me to follow him? Just in case?"

"Nah," said Steve Maya. "Maybe we'll get really lucky, and he won't come back this time."

191

20

ELLA, I, AND THE GREATEST POET SINCE SHAKESPEARE HIT THE MEAN STREETS OF MANHATTAN

Hand in hand, Ella and I followed Stu Wolff, the Bard of Lower Manhattan, into the dark and treacherous night. My cape swirled behind me as we walked. Except for the garbage and traffic, it was like following Heathcliff out on the moors.

Ella squashed my fingers every time we crossed a street, as though we were about to fling ourselves over a cliff and into the cold embrace of the sea. This was slightly less distracting than the way she went rigid whenever anyone suddenly loomed out of the shadows.

"Will you please chill out?" I whispered. "We're going to lose him if you keep slowing down like that."

Ella was watching everything at once, but I was trying to keep my eyes on the tall, thin figure several yards ahead of us. The darkness and rain made him come and go like a ghost.

"I'd rather lose him than lose my life," Ella muttered darkly.

Those were not idle words. Stu Wolff might not exactly be a man of the people at home—unless you mean the people who drive $50,000 cars—but turn him loose on the streets of the Lower West Side and he went straight for every blackened window with a Bud sign hanging in it.

Nonetheless, I barely heard her. My mind was leaping ahead to the moment when we finally caught up with Stu. Would he still be angry, or would the walk have cooled him off? Would he tell us what the argument was about? Would he ask for my advice? Maybe he'd take us for a coffee at one of his favorite cafés. I could see the three of us walking into a room filled with plants and mirrors and people wearing clothes with names (Gucci, Armani, Ralph Lauren . . .). Stu asked for his usual table. "Certainly, Mr. Wolff," cooed the waiter. A silence fell on the sophisticated New Yorkers as we passed among them. "Look who it is . . . ," they whispered. "It's Stu Wolff. . . . But who are those girls with him?"

Ella moved even closer as we trudged across Sixth Avenue for the third time. I wasn't sure if it was for warmth or protection.

"Where do you think he's going?" she whispered nervously.

"God knows," I whispered back—which put God in the minority. Not only was it pretty obvious that Stu had no destination, it seemed pretty likely from the number of times we came back to the same places that he wasn't always sure where he was.

I wasn't always sure where we were either. I'd recognized Chinatown (because of all the restaurants and Chinese people), the East Village (because we walked right past my dad's building), and the West Village (because of all the out-of-towners), but not everywhere we went was on the tourist maps, or someplace where my parents used to take me to eat, or the street that was home to my father and his dog.

Stu lurched unexpectedly to the right.

"Let's walk a little faster," Ella whispered. "We don't want to lose him."

I couldn't have agreed with her more. You wouldn't think it was possible in the city that never sleeps, but once we left the bright lights and heavy traffic of Sixth Avenue behind, the streets were pretty bleak and desolate. Figures rustled in the shadows like rats. Every sudden noise sounded like a threat.

"We won't lose him," I reassured Ella—and myself. "He can't even walk straight."

We turned the corner. And stopped.

"Where's he gone?" whispered Ella.

I squinted into the darkness. There were cans and bags and boxes of garbage piled up along the curb, and the wheel of a bicycle chained to a lamppost, but, aside from that, the narrow street of warehouses and lofts was empty. I wasn't worried though. It wasn't the first time Stu had disappeared in front of our eyes.

"He must have gone in somewhere again," I said. That was Stu's trick, suddenly vanishing through a door.

Ella shook her head. "Where would he go? There aren't any bars."

"Well, maybe he didn't go into a bar this time," I said

a little defensively. "Maybe he knows someone who lives here."

When I used to imagine what the Greatest Poet Since Shakespeare did in his spare time, I always pictured him watching sunsets and gazing into the depthless sky, his mind filled with cosmic questions and universal truths, not fighting or drinking beer—but so far tonight he'd done nothing else.

Ella pressed her lips together. "Nobody lives here," she said. "Not inside." She looked over at me. "I'm really getting scared being out here alone, Lola."

"But we're not alone," I reminded her. "We're with an adult."

"Aside from the fact that he isn't actually with us," said Ella. "Stu Wolff isn't actually an adult either; he's a rock-and-roll star."

As thunderstruck as I was by this unexpected display of disloyalty, I decided not to say anything. Later, when we were talking and laughing with Stu, I knew she'd regret those callous words.

"Well, whatever he is, we have to find him," I said diplomatically.

We started walking again, cautiously, taking small, tentative steps as though tiptoeing through a minefield. There were no bars, no coffee shops, not even an alleyway Stu might have cut through.

We stopped when we reached the next corner. Ahead of us, in all directions, were more streets just like the one we were on.

Ella sighed. "We *have* lost him." She didn't sound as disappointed as you might think.

"It's impossible," I argued. "He was right in front of us."

"Well, he's not in front of us now," said Ella. "All that's in front of us is uncollected garbage."

We were both so tired, so wet, and so hungry—and so disappointed—that it might have turned into a real argument if we hadn't been successfully diverted at that moment.

Someone—or something—groaned.

Ella practically jumped in my arms—which saved me the trouble of trying to jump into hers.

"What was that?" she hissed. I'd never seen her eyes that big. She looked really beautiful, if half-drowned.

I had to get my own heart out of my throat before I could speak. "I don't know," I whispered back. "Maybe it was a cat." Or a rat.

Clutching each other, we looked up and down the street again. But there was still nothing to see.

"Umprrgh . . . ," moaned the empty night.

Ella's nails dug into my arm. "That's not a cat."

It didn't sound much like a rat either. I pointed across the road and back the way we'd come. "I think it came from over there," I said into her ear.

The night moaned again. Painfully. Tragically. Without a shred of hope.

"It must be Stu!" I pulled on her arm. "Come on. It sounds like he's hurt."

Instead of moving forward, as I'd intended, I stayed

196

where I was, much in the way I had stayed where I was when my heel got caught in the grate. Ella wasn't budging.

"If he's hurt, then someone hurt him," said Ella in her Miss Totally Reasonable voice.

"Maybe you should be a detective when you grow up," I suggested acidly.

Ella still wouldn't move. "And maybe *you* should be a kamikaze pilot."

A garbage can crashed to the ground, the sound echoing through the vacant streets. Both of us jumped, but Ella jumped higher.

"Look!" My voice was low but urgent. "I was right. It did come from over there."

A head had appeared among the plastic bags and cans. A hand clawed the air. I was sure I heard a strangled cry for help.

Without another word—without any thought for my own safety—I let go of Ella and raced toward the hand.

"Lola!" screamed Ella, but she was already running after me over the cobbles.

We reached the fallen garbage can just in time to see the Greatest Poet Since Shakespeare throw up all over the sidewalk.

21

THE ADULT AMONG US

Ella and I stared at the huddled form of Stu Wolff as he crouched in the gutter like a Shakespearean king brought to his knees by the cruel twistings of Fate. I'd always suspected Stu Wolff was not just a genius but a tragic hero of the stature of Hamlet or Lear, and here was my proof.

Stu was propped between the toppled garbage can and a mound of plastic bags. A couple of the bags had split open, and there were colored strings and shredded paper clinging to him. The way he was sitting, he didn't seem to have bones. Besides the vomit splattered down his shirt, and the strings, and the shredded paper, he was liberally decorated with organic waste. Either he'd been in the can when it fell, or he'd been under it.

"We have to get him inside," I said. "So we can clean him up a little."

"You mean sober him up, don't you?" said Ella.

She was definitely getting better at saying what she meant.

The word "sober" must have triggered something

in the part of Stu Wolff's brain that wasn't paralyzed by alcohol. His eyes focused on us for the first time.

"I need a drink," he announced with remarkable clarity. Causing a small landslide of egg shells and fruit peels, he started to get to his feet. "I need a drink now."

Having seen every Sidhartha video at least a million times, I can tell you that watching Stu Wolff on-stage is like watching the gods dance. His movements are quick and graceful and awesome in their sensuality. But he wasn't on-stage now. He pitched forward, stumbling uncontrollably. He might really have hurt himself this time, but Ella and I were there to break his fall.

"Oomph!" the three of us gasped as one.

Ella pulled her head back, a stricken look on her face. "Omigod, his breath . . . he smells like a backed-up drain."

I tilted my own head slightly out of range of Stu's breathing. "How can you be so crass?" I demanded. "Can't you recognize a man who's haunted by demons when you see him? Can't you tell he's in cosmic pain?"

"What I can tell is that he's drunk," said Ella. To hear her, you'd think she was an expert on drunks. "And that he's puked all over himself," she added unkindly.

Stu managed a few shaky steps forward. "I'm going," he announced. "I'm going to get a drink."

"Hold on to him!" I ordered, grabbing hold of him myself. "Don't let him get away!"

Stu Wolff struggled to free himself from our hands.

"A drink!" he roared. "My kingdom for a drink!"

199

And then he suddenly stopped struggling and started laughing. "My kingdom!" he choked out between hoots of laughter. "My f—in' kingdom!" He turned to me, but I'm not really sure that he actually saw me. "You want my f—in' kingdom? You want all the fame and money? You want the f—in' fans? You can have it. You can have the whole f—in' thing. Just get me a drink!"

I wasn't too thrilled with hearing Ella and myself described as "f—in' fans," but I was willing to make allowances for the evil effects of alcohol.

I took advantage of this sudden good mood to slip my arm through his. Without my having to tell her, Ella did the same.

"A coffee," I shouted. "We're going to get you a coffee!"

"A drink!" bellowed Stu. "I want a drink!"

"We're going to get you a drink," said Ella. Unlike Stu Wolff and me, Ella wasn't screaming. She was speaking in the soft, coaxing voice of a mother reasoning with a little kid. "Just come with us, and we'll get you a drink."

To my surprise, Stu stopped screaming and laughing. "A drink," he repeated, nodding compliantly. "We're going to get a drink."

Holding Stu up between us, Ella and I started to walk.

"Where are we going?" Stu demanded after a few yards. "Where are you taking me?"

"For a drink," said Ella, her voice as soothing as the sound of the sea. "We're taking you for a drink."

Stu stopped so suddenly that the three of us knocked

into a lamppost. It was an effort, you could see that, but this time he was definitely looking at us.

"Hey," said Stu, his eyes darting back and forth between us. "Hey, did Steve send you? Are you friends of Steve?"

"Of course not." I gave him a tug. "We're *your* friends, not Steve's."

He tugged me back.

"You're Steve's friends," he said. "Well, I'm not going back with you. I know your game. You tell Steve they'll be selling ice cream in hell before I go anywhere with him again." He listed forward. He seemed to be trying to smile. "You tell him that."

Ella patted his shoulder. "We're not Steve's friends, Stu," she practically crooned. "We're *your* friends. Remember?" Ever so gently, she pulled on his arm. "We're *your* friends."

"We're *your* friends," Stu repeated. He thought about this for a second. "You're *my* friends?"

Ella nodded. "That's right, we're *your* friends. We're going to take you for a drink."

"*My* friends . . . *my* friends . . . ," he chanted as we dragged him along. "*My* friends . . . we're going for a drink. . . ." And then he made one of his sudden stops. "Who are you?" He was shouting again. "You're not my friends. I don't have any friends." He started laughing again. "Not unless they want something from me. What do you want?"

I was too traumatized by these mood swings to answer, but Ella seemed unfazed.

"We don't want anything," she assured him, coaxing him on. "We just want to buy you a drink."

I adjusted my grip as we staggered down the street. "That's Ella," I explained to Stu. "And I'm Lola."

He stopped again.

"Well, why didn't you say so?" He smiled. More or less. "My name's Stu." He stuck out a hand.

It was the moment I'd been waiting for all my young life. Eat sand, Carla Santini. I was about to shake Stu Wolff's hand. I let go of his left arm. Following my lead, Ella let go of his right.

Ella and I stood there, our hands outstretched, as Stu Wolff crumbled to the ground.

22

WHEN DREAMS COME TRUE

Given superhuman strength by Mother Necessity, Ella and I managed to half carry, half drag Stuart Harley Wolff through the unwelcoming streets of lower Manhattan in search of shelter from the storm-tossed night. Unfortunately, the only shelters that seemed to be open were bars. Ella didn't think a bar was a good idea, even though most of them serve coffee.

"How do you know they serve coffee?" I asked. "When have you ever been in a bar?" Mr. and Mrs. Gerard were as likely to take Ella to a bar as they were to take her to Lima to live among the poor.

"I've seen it in movies," said Ella. "Anyway, they'd throw us out because we're too young, and he can't be trusted to order coffee by himself."

The more we walked, the more Stu talked. His conversation shifted from politics to music to family and friends, without any awkward transitions. People owed him money. He owed people money. The IRS was after him. Several women were after him. His father wanted him to cut his hair. His mother wanted him to settle down. His agent was a thief. His manager was a liar.

Steve Maya was a backstabbing traitor. Everyone he knew was out for what they could get.

"It's a crime," Stu suddenly screamed, more or less apropros of nothing. "It's a crime, and everybody knows it's a crime, but no one will do anything about it."

I'd been so busy trying to imprint every detail of what was happening in my memory that I'd lost track of what he was saying.

"Now what's he talking about?" I asked Ella.

She grunted as Stu missed his footing and shoved her into a wall. "Nothing," said Ella. "He's just rambling incoherently. And, anyway, who cares? I just want to get inside before I drown."

Perhaps hearing the staggering lack of concern for him in Ella's voice, Stu straightened up. "Where are you taking me?" he demanded with disarming lucidity.

"We told you," Ella told him again. "We're taking you to get a drink. Remember? We're taking you for a drink."

Stu nodded. "A drink. Let's get a drink." He held up one hand. "But first I have to take a leak."

I have to admit that I was a little flummoxed by this announcement, but once again Ella rose to the occasion with competence and calm.

She pointed to the alley on our left. "Go down there," she ordered. "We'll wait for you here."

Out of respect for the privacy required by a genius— and because neither of us wanted to see more than we had to—we turned our backs while he shuffled into the dark.

I couldn't speak. My heart was too full for mere words. I had my wish: I was with Stu Wolff. True, he was more in my arms than I was in his, but I was still with him. I was beyond being just ecstatically happy; I was sitting with the gods. I was sure that once we got some coffee in him, Stu would become the man of truth, passion, and unflagging courage that I knew him to be.

"What's taking him so long?" whispered Ella, her eyes on the shadows swaying around us.

I glanced over my shoulder, just to make sure Stu was okay. He was sitting on the ground with his legs stretched in front of him and his chin on his chest.

"Oh, God!" I cried. "He's passed out. Do you think he could have been hurt when he fell? Maybe he has a concussion."

"He's going to feel like he has a concussion when he wakes up tomorrow," said Ella, as we marched down the alley to retrieve our charge. "He's going to have the hangover from hell."

Side by side, we bent over Stu. I was trying to make sure that his fine and noble heart was still beating, but Ella started slapping his face.

"Stu!" she called. *Slapslapslap.* "Stu, wake up. We're going for a drink."

I was really intrigued. I'd never seen this Four-Star-General side of Ella before.

"Where did you learn to do that?" I asked.

"Movies," said Ella.

Stu opened his eyes, staring at us in an almost

catatonic silence for a few seconds, much as a man might stare at angels.

"Who are you?" he demanded. "Where are you taking me?"

"You remember us," said Ella. "It's Ella and Lola. We're your friends." We hauled him to his feet. "We're taking you for a drink."

It felt as though we'd been walking through the hostile, darkling night for hours before we stumbled upon a place of refuge, safe from the ravages of the storm and the possibility of cold-blooded murder.

We found a café.

That is, it said it was a café. But if you, like I, think of a café as being small but elegant, French and atmospheric—the kind of place where one might write a poem to order an espresso—then the Purity Café was a diner. From the looks of it, it had probably been a diner for about fifty years.

I wiped a circle of dirt and steam from the window and peered inside. I could see booths, a Formica counter, a chrome and glass fridge, and, strung above the griddle, dulled red foil letters that spelled out MERRY MAS.

I stepped back so Ella could see. "What do you think?"

Preparatory to taking him in among the people, Ella was wiping the vomit from Stu's shirt with a tissue and didn't bother to look.

"So long as there aren't armed men inside holding everyone hostage, I think it's great," said Ella. "I just want to sit down."

She was definitely surprising me, I have to admit it. The Ella I met when I first moved to Deadwood would have been in tears by now, running from corner to corner, looking for a public phone that was working so she could call home collect.

"Come on," said Stu, lurching at the door. "I really need a drink."

The wall that ran along the booths was covered with mirrors. As we stepped into the steamy warmth of the Purity Café, I could see three figures staring back at us over the clutch of condiments that graced each table. Two teenage girls in bedraggled party gear and a drunken twenty-nine-year-old man with string and shredded paper clinging to him, and vomit all over his boots. We looked like people routinely picked up by the cops.

The other customers of the Purity Café, glancing up from their drinks and food, saw what I saw. You could practically hear them praying that we wouldn't sit near them.

"Get him into a booth," ordered Ella as the waitress bore down on us. "Quick, before she sees his feet."

We dragged Stu to the nearest booth. I got in first and pulled him after me.

As soon as he hit the fake leather seat, Stu started talking.

"Everybody wants something from me," he informed us again. "Even people I don't know. Everybody thinks they own me."

The waitress stopped by our table, pad in hand. If this were Deadwood, the sight of us would have put her into cardiac arrest by now. But this wasn't Deadwood; it was New York. She had the jaded, seen-it-all air of the waitress in a depressing play. She looked at Stu.

"What'll it be?"

"You think I have any real friends?" Stu asked her. "None of my friends give two cents about me. If I lost everything tomorrow, I'd never see any of them again."

Her eyes fell on his sodden silk shirt with the bits of vomit Ella hadn't been able to get off, and tentacles of paper and string.

"You're in luck then," the waitress told him. "'Cause it looks like you have lost everything."

"We'll just have coffee," said Ella politely.

"Not me," said Stu. "I'll have a boilermaker and a deluxe hamburger platter, with a large side of onion rings."

Ella and I exchanged a look of panic. We didn't have enough money for a deluxe hamburger platter and a large side of onion rings.

"This isn't a bar," said the waitress. "How do you want your patty?"

Ella leaned across the table and touched Stu's hand. "You're not really hungry, are you?" she inquired gently. "Why don't you just have a coffee for now?" She smiled encouragingly. "Or mineral water. Mineral water would be better than coffee."

Stu acted like he hadn't heard her. "Rare," he ordered. "Swiss cheese."

Ella turned her smile on the waitress. "Just bring him a coffee," she said sweetly. She winked. "He isn't really up to a meal right now."

Stu stood up. He'd heard her that time.

"I want a deluxe hamburger platter and onion rings!" he bellowed. "And I want it now!"

The waitress raised one eyebrow. "You two better keep him in line," she warned. "The boss won't stand for any nonsense."

I looked over at the heavyset man behind the counter. The one talking to the two cops who were eating doughnuts and drinking coffee. He seemed to be deeply engrossed in their conversation, but all the time he was glancing around the room. His eyes met mine for one very long second, and then he laughed.

"Don't worry," Ella promised. "He's all right. He just had a little too much to drink."

After the waitress shuffled off, Stu fell back in his seat and turned on Ella and me.

"What do you want?" he demanded. He seemed a little obsessed with this question. "Autographs? Money? A quick roll in the hay?"

A quick roll in the hay?

I stared at him, agog. Was this the poet whose words of light had lit my darkest days; the genius whose

209

intuition and wisdom had so inspired me? I was shocked, I admit it. Shocked and disappointed. Stu Wolff was a spiritual being. He was supposed to be above things like rolling in the hay.

Ella's treacherous words repeated themselves in my mind. *Stu Wolff's not an adult; he's a rock-and-roll star. . . . Stu Wolff's not an adult; he's a rock-and-roll star. . . .*

"We don't want anything," I enunciated carefully into his ear. "We're trying to help you."

Stu laughed. It was a laugh of torment and pain.

"You don't want anything? Well, that sets a new president, doesn't it?"

"Precedent," I automatically corrected.

Stu wasn't listening. He was still talking.

"What are you two, aliens or something?" He listed to the left, knocking over the menu propped against the napkin holder. "Hey!" he shouted to the other customers. "Hey! These girls are from another planet!"

The waitress and the counterman looked over. The two tired-looking workmen in the next booth looked over. The women at the back looked over. The cops looked over, too.

Ella leaned across the table again and put both her hands on Stu's. "Shhhh . . . ," Ella calmed him. "You have to be quiet or they'll throw us out."

Stu pulled roughly away. "Why? I don't *have* to be anything. I have three gold records. I can do what I want."

One of the cops looked over again.

Genetics is a complicated thing. As different as I am from Karen Kapok, when I opened my mouth I sounded just like my mother.

"No, you can't," I told him firmly. "You're making a spectacle of yourself."

It didn't work when my mother told me I was making a spectacle of myself, and it didn't work with Stu either.

"But I am a spectacle," he announced to the Purity Café in a working-the-stadium roar. "You think I'm a regular guy? I'm not a regular guy."

"Shhh!!" I hissed. I didn't have Ella's patience.

Stu didn't s*hhh.*

"I'm a three-ring circus," he boomed on. "You think anybody knows me? Nobody knows me!" He knocked the bowl of sugar packets off the table. "I don't even know myself."

I gave Ella a look. "Didn't I tell you?" I whispered. "He's a tortured soul."

The waitress arrived with our coffees. "Food's coming," she muttered. The cop who was eating the powdered doughnut was watching her over his shoulder.

Ella squashed her mouth into a line. "Torture's involved," she agreed. She shook her head sadly. "But it makes you think, doesn't it? I mean, why shouldn't he be happy? He has everything he could possibly want. . . ."

No, he didn't.

"What's this?" Stu spluttered as the waitress set a cup in front of him. "This isn't a boilermaker."

"It's coffee," said the waitress. "I told you before, this is a restaurant, not a bar."

Before I could stop him, Stu was on his feet and pushing past the waitress. "I have to go to the john," he announced loudly. "I expect that to be a boilermaker by the time I get back."

23

THINGS TAKE A TURN FOR THE WORSE

While Stu was away, Ella and I congratulated ourselves on how well everything was working out.

"Can you believe it, El?" I could barely control my excitement. "You and I are having coffee with Stu Wolff!" I'd never let Carla Santini live this down.

A frown crossed Ella's face. "I wish he were sober, though. It's so hard talking to someone who's drunk."

As if she'd had a lot of experience talking to drunks. Ella had less than I did, and the only time I've seen either of my parents really wasted was the Christmas my father hit the eggnog too hard and danced into the tree. It was quite a sight. But my father hadn't behaved like Stu. My father had been happy. He was still laughing as he took broken bits of Christmas ball from his hair.

"I wish he were, too," I admitted. "I have so many questions I want to ask him about his work."

Ella tentatively sipped her coffee. "I wonder why he *is* so unhappy," she mused. "You'd think he'd be the happiest guy in the world."

I'd tried to explain to Ella that artists aren't like

ordinary people, but she clearly hadn't understood. Not that I blamed her. Mr. and Mrs. Gerard think suffering is when their lawn gets crabgrass or the deli runs out of Brie.

"You just don't understand the artistic soul," I said. But, fortunately, I did. And I knew Stu's soul almost as well as I knew my own. There wasn't a line he'd written that wasn't burned into my memory and etched into my heart. "The artistic soul can never be happy. It creates through anguish and pain. That's probably why he drank so much." My face clouded with empathy. "He has to numb the intensity of his feelings. All true geniuses do."

Ella, of course, was radically impressed by my explanation. She looked over her shoulder toward the restrooms.

"You know," she said, "he's been in there awhile. I hope he's all right."

The counterman, the waitress, and the cops were all looking toward the restrooms, too.

Ella turned back to me. "Do you think he's passed out again?"

"At least we know that he's safe if he has," I answered, slightly distracted for the moment. I was watching the cops push their cups away. The one with powdered sugar on his chin got to his feet and strolled toward the door. I didn't like the way he glanced over at me and Ella as he stepped into the street. It suddenly occurred to me that Ella's concern about her mother's protectiveness might be justified. What if Mrs. Gerard had called my house to check on Ella after all? A person with far less imagination than I could easily picture what would have happened next. The shrieking; the tears; the phone calls; the overwrought conversation with the police . . .

As casually as a person who is dripping all over could, I glanced toward the street again. The patrol car was parked on a yellow line right out front. The police officer was sitting inside, talking on the radio. I wished I could read his lips. Was he saying, "That's right, one has blond hair, and the other one's a redhead"?

My euphoria had vanished. It would be just my luck to end up not in Stu Wolff's embrace but in the strong arms of the law.

The waitress materialized with Stu's order and the coffeepot. "Your friend's takin' a long time," she said conversationally as she refilled our cups. "I think one of you better go check on him before the boss does."

As one, Ella and I looked toward the boss. He was leaning between a plastic bottle of ketchup and a pitcher of milk, talking to the remaining cop, but his eyes kept darting to the restrooms.

"I'll go," I volunteered.

Nonchalant as an antelope, I walked to the back of the diner, praying that no one could hear me squelch. I slipped into the ladies' room—which was next to the men's room—and locked the door.

"Stu!" I hissed urgently. "Stu! Are you okay?"

I pressed my ear to the wall. I couldn't hear a sound.

My next move was to try banging.

"Stu!" *Bangbangbang.* "Stu, it's Lola. Answer me. Are you okay?"

The silence of a pharaoh's tomb came back at me. And that was when this really awful thought struck me like an arrow. What if Stu had gone in the john to kill himself? He was drunk, he was depressed, and he was haunted by the fear that he would never find anyone to love him for himself. Maybe he even worried (foolishly) that his career was over, now that the band was gone. Tortured geniuses are prone to suicide.

I exited the ladies' room, acting carefree and calm.

The second cop had come back and was talking to his partner. The counterman was scraping gunk from the grill. The waitress was cutting a wedge of pie. Only Ella was looking at me.

I put my hand on the doorknob of the men's room, and turned it gently. It was locked. I pressed my ear to the door. I couldn't hear anyone breathing. My stomach began to churn as I pictured the crumpled form on the floor—the eyes open, the lips slightly parted, the handsome face blank, the once great mind as gone as yesterday. A soft cry of pain escaped me. I turned back to the diner, unsure of what to do.

A dark figure was passing in front of the restaurant. Slowly and uncertainly. Almost stumbling, it braced itself against the window for a second. Joy, relief, and total panic all surged through me at once. It was Stuart Harley Wolff! He must have found a way out the back. No mean feat for a man in his condition.

I raced to our booth and grabbed my things. "Come on," I said. "We have to go."

"But Stu—"

"Now!" I gave her a yank. "He got out!"

Ella scrambled to her feet. "What about the bill?"

The bill! The greatest talent of our times was staggering unhappily through the tempest-tossed night, and all Ella could think about was the bill! Her parents really have a lot to answer for.

I picked up the check and pretended to examine it carefully. The deluxe hamburger platter was $5.95. The large onion rings was another $2.50. The coffees were nearly $3.00.

"Put whatever you have on the table," I ordered. I put down my five-dollar bill and fifty-eight cents.

Ella put down $1.40. "You had the rest of my money," said Ella. And then, in case I'd overlooked the obvious, she added, "We don't have enough."

One of the cops had disappeared; the other was watching us in the mirror behind the counter.

I got a firm grip on Ella's arm. "Just walk to the door like nothing's wrong," I whispered.

"And then what?" she whispered back.

"Then run."

It would have worked, I'm sure it would have. But we never got a chance to run. The cop got up as we started walking; he blocked our way to the door.

"Not so fast," he said, friendly and kindly. "I want to ask you two a couple of questions."

"Now?" I asked, feigning panic and urgency. "I'm afraid we're in a hurry. Our friend—" I tried to push past him.

He took each of us gently but firmly by the arm.

"Don't worry about your friend," said the cop. "He's going to be just fine."

24

OH, WHAT A TANGLED WEB I'D WOVEN

I will never forget that ride to the precinct house. The streets were dark and blurred with rain; the blue lights flashed; the neon signs shone feebly through the storm; the windshield wipers whispered like demons. Given her views on being driven home in a patrol car, I'd expected Ella to feel equally strongly about being driven to the precinct house in a patrol car, but she sat calmly in the back seat between me and the dozing Stuart Wolff, humming a Sidhartha song under her breath.

I was the one who was upset. It was obvious that Officer Lentigo didn't believe my story. Which was that we were eighteen-year-old N.Y.U. students, that we were out on a date with Stu and another guy, that the other guy had gone to get his car, and that we'd taken Stu to the diner to sober him up a little while we waited.

"You know what college guys are like," I'd joked.

"He looks a little old to be in college," said Officer Lentigo.

I laughed, indulgently. "He's getting his master's in literature."

Officer Lentigo didn't so much as crack a smile. "You got some ID?" he asked.

It was then that Officer Grimkin came back with Stu, and Officer Lentigo decided to take us all back to the precinct to call our folks.

The desk sergeant recognized Stu the minute he leaned against the front desk, demanding a drink, under the misapprehension that he'd finally found a bar.

"Hey," said the sergeant. "I know this guy." He wagged his pen at Stu. "Aren't you a singer?"

It was as if—like Sleeping Beauty kissed by the Prince—Stu had been under a spell that had finally been broken. He looked around, blinking in confusion. "What's going on?"

The sergeant shook his head emphatically. "Yeah, you are a singer." He looked over at Officers Lentigo and Grimkin. "Janellen's got pictures of him all over her walls," he explained.

"Lucky her," said Officer Grimkin.

"I thought you told me he was a grad student," Officer Lentigo said to me.

"That, too," I said.

Perhaps realizing that his fellow officers weren't as impressed by Janellen's wall decorations as they might have been, the sergeant became more businesslike.

"Okay," he said brusquely. "Let's have some names, addresses, and telephone numbers." He pointed his pen at Stu again. "You first."

"Stuart Harley Wolff," said Stu immediately. He frowned. "Are we being arrested?"

"Not yet," said the sergeant. "Address and phone?"

Stu gave him his address and number, and then turned his frown on me and Ella. "Are we together? Who are you?"

The sergeant tapped on the desk with his pen. "I was just about to ask them the same thing."

Now, I thought, was the moment when Ella would lose it. The moment when she had to put the N.Y.P.D. in touch with Marilyn Gerard. I turned to give her a smile of support, but to my surprise Ella wasn't looking at me. She was looking at the desk sergeant.

"Ella Gerard, 58 Birch Hollow Road, Dellwood, New Jersey, 201-238-4917," she said almost regally. You'd think she did this kind of thing all the time.

Then everyone looked at me.

"Lola Cep," I said. I'd been giving this moment a lot of thought on the drive over; I didn't hesitate for a nanosecond. The last thing I needed was for the police to wake up Karen Kapok in the middle of the night. Besides, what could my mother do? No one could expect her to drive down in a hurricane with her two little daughters, could they? Tragedy could only result from such a rash action. I was doing her a favor. My father could tell her—later. He isn't as volatile as my mother. "My father's address is 311 Second Avenue, Apartment F, 460-5517."

I felt, rather than saw, Ella's expression change from one of princessly serenity to cataclysmic horror.

"Okay," said Officer Lentigo. "Why don't you two take the literature student here, and go sit down while I make some calls."

I don't know if it was all the walking in the rain or the sobering effect of being taken in by the cops, but though Stu was kind of dazed, he definitely wasn't as drunk as he'd been earlier. Walking almost steadily, he followed us to the row of chairs against the wall.

Ella didn't seem to notice him. Her calm and cool was totally gone. She turned on me.

"What's wrong with you?" she hissed. "Why did you lie like that? Don't you think they're going to find out that your father doesn't live on Second Avenue?"

Stu tapped her on the shoulder. "Excuse me," he said, obviously struggling to clear his head, "but what's going on? Who are you two?"

I'd been so absorbed in what was happening that I'd forgotten Ella thought my father was a road statistic. Stress wreaks havoc with delicate fabrications. That's one fact of life that I've learned. Another is that the best defense is a quick offense.

I ignored Stu, too.

"What's with you?" I snapped at Ella. "All of a sudden you're giving your address and phone number to the first policeman who asks for it. How come you're not afraid of what your parents are going to say?"

"I'm resigned to my fate," said Ella rather dramatically. She shrugged. "Besides, what's the use of more lies? They're going to find out one way or another." She shrugged again. "At least this'll be something to tell our grandchildren, won't it?" She forgot her outrage enough to smile. "The only things my parents will have to tell their grandchildren are their golf handicaps."

It really had been quite a day. I could hardly believe I was hearing this from Ella Gerard, perfect daughter of perfect parents. Her true soul and spirit were finally beginning to emerge.

Maybe a little too much.

Ella folded her arms in front of her. "So," she said. "Why did you lie?"

It was time, I could tell, to unleash the truth. I turned my eyes on the rich mix of life that was milling around the front desk while I answered.

"I didn't lie," I said quietly as some guy in handcuffs was dragged down the hall. "My father does live on Second Avenue. He has a rent-controlled apartment and a dog named Negus."

Stu cleared his throat. "Look," he said, "this is really fascinating, but could one of you please tell me what happened? The last thing I remember is throwing a CD at Steve." He made a face. "And I only remember that vaguely."

But Ella was no longer interested in Stu. She leaned close to me. "You told me your father died in a motorcycle accident," she said very loudly and clearly.

I looked at her out of the corner of my eye. "All right," I gave in. "So I exaggerated a little."

She almost laughed. "You exaggerated a little? You killed off your own father, and you call that exaggerating a little?" Her gestapo gaze bored into the side of my head. "What do you call exaggerating a lot?"

"Look," I said, still trying to avoid direct eye contact. "Can't we talk about this later? Don't you think we should tell Stu what happened first?"

The old Ella would have backed down instantly. She would have apologized for being rude and, remembering all the rules about politeness and manners instilled in her by her parents, would have started being helpful to Stu. But the new Ella couldn't have cared less.

She shook her head. "I think you should tell me what happened. Why did you say that your father was dead?"

I shrugged. "I had a reason."

"Well, that's a start," said Ella. "And what, pray tell, was that?"

Pray tell? Since when had Ella started stealing my lines?

Stu's head moved back and forth between us as though he were watching a tennis match.

Before I could answer, Ella held up a hand. "And don't tell me you lied because he's a criminal or was tragically maimed rescuing a baby from a burning building either," she warned me. "This time I want the truth."

224

"The truth?"

"Yes," said Ella. "The truth. You do remember what that is, don't you?"

Sure, I thought, *it's boring.*

"Were we in a diner?" asked Stu. "I have this image of old Christmas decorations. . . ."

Ella stopped staring at me. Temporarily. "If you could just hold on a minute," she said, "I'd be happy to explain. But right now I'm talking to *her*." She turned back to me as she said *her.*

Stu turned to me, too. "Tell her, will you? I'd like to know what's going on."

I sighed. I knew I was beaten. "All right," I said. "The total truth." I looked at Stu. He had no idea who I was, and still he wasn't as hostile as Ella. I took a deep breath. "I lied because I wanted to make myself seem more interesting, that's all."

"More interesting?" repeated Ella. She glanced around the room as though taking a quick inventory, starting with the two women of the night who were standing at the front desk and ending with Stu. "We're sitting here, in a New York police station with a cultural icon, waiting for your dead father to show up, and you want to be more interesting? More interesting than what?"

"You don't understand," I said—sadly, as a person used to being misunderstood would. "It was a new town, a new school . . ."

"I understand," said Stu. "I think."

I immediately felt less defensive. I believed him. If anyone could understand, I was pretty sure he, a true artist and kindred spirit, could.

"It wasn't intentional," I told Stu. "It just came out like that and then I couldn't change it." I smiled dauntedly. "I mean, if I'd been thinking more clearly I'd have had him move to Tibet or something."

"Tibet's good," said Stu. "It's mystic, and nobody's going to go look for him there."

Ella, however, is more attached to a narrow, pedestrian concept of truth.

"So were they really married?" asked Ella. "Or did you make that up, too?"

"Of course I didn't make that up. They really loved— love—each other." This, too, was true. My parents are largely incompatible, but they're really good friends. "He just didn't die in a road accident, that's all." I gave Ella an accusatory look. "I don't lie about fundamentals," I explained, not hiding my hurt. "Only minor details."

But Ella was stuck in the minor details.

"What about Elk?" she persisted. "Where's he?"

I kept my eyes on Stu. "California."

Ella shook her head. "This is incredible," she said. "I feel like I'm in a movie or something." She smiled bittersweetly. *The Life and Times of Lola Cep.*

"You know," said Stu, who was much less self-obsessed when relatively sober than when relatively not, "I really would like to know what's going on."

Nor was he the only one. Even as I was sitting there with both Ella and Stu staring at me expectantly, the main door opened and a large mixed-breed dog walked in, followed by a thin, fair-haired man in faded jeans and a black leather jacket, his hair close-cropped and a diamond stud in one ear. The man looked around uneasily.

"You think that's Marsh Foreman?" whispered Ella.

The man's eyes fell on Ella, Stu, and me.

"Mary!" cried my father. "What the hell's going on?"

As the rain continued to fall on the dark, heartless streets, the six of us gathered around Officer Lentigo's cluttered desk and I told our tale. Succinctly, but with passion and raw honesty. I told how desperate Ella and I had been to see Sidhartha's last concert, but our parents, insensitive to the intensity of our needs and feelings, refused to let us go. How we tried so hard but couldn't get tickets. How we decided to crash the party rather than have our dreams forever denied. How everything had gone so incredibly wrong, as though the Fates themselves were pulling the strings. How we'd seen Stu storm out of the Soho loft and followed him to make sure he didn't come to any harm. It was a slightly edited version. I didn't mention Carla Santini, and I didn't mention telling Ella that my father had been dead for sixteen years—I didn't want to complicate it too much.

I'd been right to resurrect my father rather than wake

up my mother. My mother would have interrupted my story every sentence or two to ask annoying questions—like, how did you know about the party? or, where did you get that dress?—but my father only interrupted once to say, "But I said I'd take you to the concert," and was satisfied with my explanation of our desperate desire to get to the party without an escort. He could understand; he'd been young once, too.

My father kept shaking his head while I talked, but Officers Lentigo and Grimkin and Stu Wolff, riveted by my story, were motionless and staring.

"I know I should be furious," said my father when we were through. He sighed, looking at me with a mixture of paternal love and paternal frustration. "But I'm not up to fury right now. I'm just thankful nothing worse happened."

Officers Lentigo and Grimkin were stern but not unkind. They agreed we were lucky they'd become interested in us before someone less savory did.

Stu said, "Well, now that that's settled, does anyone want to go to a party with me?"

My mother would have said "No." She has a very rigid sense of justice.

My father looked at me and Ella. "Oh, what the hell," said my father. "Is it okay if we bring the dog?"

25

ALL'S WELL THAT ENDS WELL

"All right," said Ella softly as we drove to Stu's loft in my father's car, "I'm prepared to forgive you."

How generous, I thought. She hadn't ruined Eliza's ball gown. She didn't have to face Mrs. Baggoli. She didn't have to face Karen Kapok. She didn't even have to face Marilyn and Jim Gerard—there'd been no one home when Officer Lentigo called, and the answering machine hadn't been on. She didn't really have anything to forgive me for. I didn't say anything though. So far, things were working out better than even I could have hoped. I didn't want to rock the boat.

Ella's face was stern in the shimmering shadows. "But you have to promise you'll never lie to me again," said Ella. "You know what my mother always says: 'You can trust a thief but never a liar.'"

Personally, that seemed a bit harsh to me. I mean, sure I'd elaborated on dull reality a little, but I never lied about anything important. I would never let Ella down. I would never betray her. I would never say I was her friend and then steal her boyfriend, the way some people would.

"I promise," I said solemnly. "I'll never lie again—not even about things that aren't important. I've learned the error of my ways."

"Thank God for that," said Ella, but I made out more than relief in her expression. She was as happy as I was. We'd done it! We were going to arrive at the Sidhartha party with Stu Wolff. Carla Santini was going to have a herd of cows!

In the front seat, Stu and my father were talking about my father's picture books. Stu had recognized my father's name. His niece was a big fan of my father's rabbits.

I leaned back against the hairs that cover the back seat of my father's car, and smiled. "Can you wait to see Carla's face when we walk in?" I asked softly. "Or what?"

Ella grinned back. "No, I can't. If I wasn't so wet and hungry and half-crippled I wouldn't believe it was going to happen." She winked. "All's well that ends well," said Ella.

You wouldn't have been able to tell it was the middle of the night from the scene in Stu's duplex loft. The party was in full swing. Even though he had enough room to house a jumbo jet, the place was packed.

Ella and I hung back in the doorway for a few seconds, our eyes trying to take it all in.

"Look over there!" Ella kept saying as she spotted

another celebrity. "Look over there! Look over there!"

"Come on," said Stu. "I'll lend you guys something dry and have those dresses cleaned and at your dad's by tomorrow afternoon."

I pinched Ella hard. "Stu Wolff's clothes!" I hissed. "We're going to be wearing Stu Wolff's clothes!"

"I'll be over there," said my father, pointing to the main bar. "I think I'd like a drink."

As we followed Stu up a spiral staircase to his bedroom, my eyes scanned the crowd of famous faces for the infamous one of Carla Santini.

"I don't see her," I whispered to Ella. "Do you?"

Ella shook her head.

Stu left us with two very worn Sidhartha T-shirts and two pairs of track pants, and went off to find my father. "Imagine meeting Calum Cep," he said. "I can't believe my luck!"

"He can't believe *his* luck?" I softly shrieked when the door shut behind him. I buried my face in the T-shirt that had so often stunk from Stu Wolff's sweat. "I feel like I've died and gone to heaven."

"Not yet," said Ella. "Not till Carla Santini sees us."

We descended the spiral staircase slowly, pausing every rung or two to survey the revelers in their designer clothes and glinting jewelry, our heads held high. What did we care that we looked freshly drowned and ready for a jog? We didn't. We were the privileged ones. We were the ones who had brought Stu back. We were the ones tripping over his pants.

We were on the last few steps when we spotted Carla. She and Alma were demurely following Mr. and Mrs. Santini as they cut a path to the door through the throng.

"Carla!" I cried. "We've been looking for you."

I saw her glance over. She didn't turn her head or scream or anything, but she did glance over. Alma glanced over, too.

And then they disappeared behind a waiter with a tray full of food.

"Did you see her face?" Ella was as delighted as I was. "I'm glad I don't have to ride home with her. She's going to be in a really bad mood."

I laughed out loud. "All's well that ends well," I said.

We all had a great time at the party, even Negus. Several people with small children recognized Negus as Buster, the hero of *My Dog, Buster* and *Buster Runs Away,* and they made a big fuss over him and stuffed him with canapés. My father and Stu discovered that they were both into climbing and talked till four in the morning about rock faces and ropes. In fact, my father enjoyed himself so much that by the time we got up on Sunday he'd more or less forgotten why we'd gone to the party in the first place. After he called my mother again, he took Ella and me to lunch, and after our dresses came back from Stu's cleaners (good as new), he drove us home.

My mother, however, had not been at the party, and had not had a good time. My mother said that if I ever pulled a stunt like that again, she'd have me lobotomized. In fact, she'd do it herself.

"Do you have any idea how worried I was when your father called?" she screamed. "Do you have any idea what could have happened to you, traipsing around Manhattan in the middle of the night? How could you lie to me like that?"

"I was desperate," I sobbed. "You didn't understand how important it was to me."

"And you don't seem to understand how important keeping you alive is to me," said my mother.

My punishment was six months of hard labor, with no chance of parole.

"I don't care what plans you've already made," raged my mother. "If I need you to baby-sit, that's what you do. Six months," she repeated. "You'll be free for your birthday." She gave me a motherly smile. "Make sure you live to enjoy it."

I promised I would. I could afford to be contrite— and generous—I was getting off lightly, and I knew it. My mother knew nothing about the dress, which I'd smuggled into the house in my bag, and that meant that Mrs. Baggoli wasn't going to know about it either. There was no way she'd be able to tell by looking at it now that it had spent Saturday in New York. I didn't get off as lightly as Ella though. Her parents were out when she got home, and the only thing they asked about Saturday was "Have a nice time at Lola's?" My mother agreed not to tell the Gerards what had happened.

"There's no point upsetting them now," said my mother. "Besides, I know Ella had nothing to do with this. She just let herself be persuaded by you. I don't think that deserves the wrath of the Gerards." It was the first time I realized that Karen Kapok probably liked Ella's parents a lot less than they liked her.

Once my mother had calmed down, I spent the rest of Sunday in a state of euphoria. I couldn't join in the family conversation. I couldn't eat. I couldn't even face my homework. I just lay on my bed, listening to Sidhartha on my stereo and planning my entrance at school the following morning. I wanted every detail straight in my head so I could stand back and enjoy my total triumph.

26

SNATCHING DEFEAT FROM THE JAWS OF VICTORY

Sam Creek arrived in his Karmann Ghia to collect me and the dress on Monday morning.

"So?" said Sam as I squashed myself into the front seat. "How'd it go? Did you manage to get in?"

"You won't believe what happened!" I said, too excited to pretend to be cool. "You just won't believe it!"

I told him what happened.

"And you should have seen my dad," I concluded. "Lots of Stu's friends knew his books. It was really weird."

Sam took his hands from the wheel for a second. "Hallelujah!" he shouted. "This is the day I've been waiting for since kindergarten, when Carla Santini used to talk me out of my dessert every lunch. I cannot wait to see her face."

He didn't have long to wait.

Ella was waiting for us in the courtyard, right outside the student lounge. In my old school, the teachers were lucky to have a faculty room, but in Deadwood even the kids have their own room. The student lounge has three walls of glass, a bunch of chairs and low tables, and a drink machine. Ella jerked her head behind her as we approached.

"Carla's already started boring everybody to death with every microscopic detail of the concert and the party," said Ella. She looked a lot different than she had just two days before. This was partly because she had her hair down, but it was more than that. She looked brighter, happier, sort of more vivid.

Sam and I looked through the wall of window. Carla Santini was holding court from the center chair, flanked by Alma, Tina, and Marcia, and surrounded by a gaggle of BTWs. She must have known Ella was waiting for me because she turned to face me and smiled.

"Uh oh," said Sam. "What's that supposed to mean?"

"What?" asked Ella, her back to Carla.

"She smiled," said Sam.

"Are you sure?" asked Ella.

The way they were carrying on, you'd think they were two Red Guards talking about Stalin. *He scratched his ear this morning. . . . Well, someone's off to the firing squad. . . .*

"She's bluffing," I said airily. "She doesn't want everyone to know she spent yesterday crying her eyes out." I grabbed both of them by the arm and steered them toward the entrance of the lounge. "Come on," I said. "Let's watch Carla Santini eat humble pie."

Everyone turned around as Ella, Sam, and I stepped into the lounge.

"Well, if it isn't the Great Pretender!" called Carla.

236

"Kill her now," muttered Sam.

The smile that had been on Carla's face since she saw us grew like a cancer. "Come to hear what the Sidhartha party was like?" she crowed.

As if she'd said something hysterically funny, the rest of them laughed.

"Why would we want to hear what you have to say?" I asked sweetly. "Ella and I were there, remember?"

This, apparently, was even funnier than what Carla had said.

Alma started shrieking hysterically. "Oh, my God!" Tears of laughter watering her mascara, she turned to Carla. "Did you hear *that*? She said they were there!"

Marcia gave me a pitying look. "You know, lying's not going to help you," she said as though she wanted to be helpful. "Everybody already knows that you didn't go." She shook her head, baffled, as many of us are, by human behavior. "How could you think you'd get away with it?" she wondered aloud. "Nobody who isn't an idiot believed you in the first place."

"That's right!" chimed in Tina. "I mean, *you*? The only way you'd get into a party like that is if you were one of the waitresses."

I stood there, taking their abuse, staring at Carla in shocked disbelief. She had no intention of eating humble pie; it wasn't on the Santini menu. She was going to lie through her teeth, and make it her word against mine.

"Don't you pretend you didn't see me!" I was calm,

but strong. I stood up straight. "I know you did." I sent a sneer in Tina's direction. "And don't you tell me the only way I'd get into a party like that is as a waitress. It just so happens that Ella and I got in *with* Stu Wolff. *After* we practically saved his life."

Carla gestured to the photographs spread out on the table in front of her. "There's the proof," she purred. In case I was too thick to get what she meant she explained. "Those are my pictures from the concert and the party. Lola isn't in one of them. But *Stu* is." Her smile was Antarctica with lipstick. "Now how could you have been saving his life, Lola, when he never left the party all night?" She made a helpless gesture to her audience. "Why isn't Lola in any of the pictures?" Her expression became sweetly sly. "It's not like she's camera shy, is it?"

Another round of laughter greeted this insightful witticism.

"Bride at the wedding, corpse at the funeral," muttered Alma.

I wanted to turn the tables on her. I wanted to say that she *had* taken a photo, but she was pretending that she hadn't. Only Ella was there. I'd promised her I wouldn't lie anymore, and I definitely wasn't going to when she could hear me.

"You're not going to get away with this," I said instead. "Ella and I were at that party. My dad and Stu are even going climbing together—sometime." When Stu got back from finding himself in India.

238

That, unfortunately, was the wrong thing to say.

Carla went off like a siren. "Your dad? But you don't have a dad, Lola. Ella's mother told my mother that your father died before you were born." She turned her lethal smile on Ella. "Isn't that true?" she asked.

It was obvious that our adventure really had changed Ella. She recovered more quickly from this sudden attack than I did.

"If you say so, it must be true," said Ella sarcastically but without strictly lying. "All I know is that Lola's father is very much alive and living on the Lower East Side."

The homeroom bell sounded.

Carla smiled. "Of course he is. He and Stu Wolff are probably climbing up some mountain in Manhattan even as we speak." She gave Ella another killer dose of smile. "Didn't I say you should come with me?"

Monday went downhill from there.

History, Spanish, and science weren't total hell because, though everyone darted knowing glances at Ella and me, and muttered among themselves, Carla wasn't in those classes with us, egging everyone else on. But in math, Ms. Pollard sent Sam to the principal for threatening to deck Morgan Liepe because he called Ella and me liars. And in English, where we had a substitute teacher because Mrs. Baggoli was taking one of her classes on a field trip and we were supposed to be writing an in-class essay, Carla passed her photographs around so everyone could see firsthand the proof that Ella and I hadn't been at the party. Hearing the hissed wisecracks and snickers, the substitute teacher periodically raised her head from the book she was reading, but as soon as she went back to it, the wisecracks and snickers would start again.

After school, Ella went home looking down, and Sam and I got the dress out of his car and snuck it back into the drama room closet. At least some things were going according to plan.

"Maybe Carla really didn't see you," said Sam as we climbed into the Karmann Ghia. "I mean, it is possible. The party was really crowded, right? And it was late."

I snorted with derision. "Oh, please . . . she saw us all right." I opened the passenger door again and freed my cape. "You should have seen her face. She looked like she'd just swallowed her tongue."

We pulled out of the parking lot.

"You should have taken your own camera with you," said Sam. He shook his head. "I mean, if you think about it, it always was a 'heads Carla wins; tails you and Ella lose' proposition. Even if she'd taken a photo of all of you together, she would never have admitted it."

"Thanks for thinking of that now," I said. I hadn't even thought about bringing a camera with us because I knew Carla would have one. The last thing I'd needed to do was lose or break my mother's Pentax on top of all my other crimes. "And anyway," I went on more pleasantly, "I do have proof. I have Stu's T-shirt."

Sam gave me a look. It was not an encouraging one.

"Have you been paying any attention to what's happening?" he asked. He sounded as though he was worried about my sanity. "So what if you have Stu Wolff's T-shirt, Lola? How are you planning to prove he gave it to you, or even that it's his?"

I opened my mouth to answer. "Well . . . I . . . uh . . ." I closed it again. Sam was right, of course. It was like agreeing to fight a duel with pistols and discovering that your opponent has a nuclear bomb. I mean, it wasn't exactly what you'd call playing by the rules. But then, as even Carla had tried to explain to me, Carla has her own rules, and everyone else has to play by them.

"People will believe me," I said firmly. I wasn't going to let Carla Santini shake my faith in all mankind. "Why would I lie about something like that?"

He winked. "Why would any of us lie, Lola?" asked Sam.

The Big Freeze had settled over Deadwood High once again. I had no opportunity to explain to anyone where my new T-shirt had come from, because no one was specifically talking to me. Or to Ella.

"Gee," said Ella as we walked to the auditorium together after English through a sea of indifference, "seems like old times, doesn't it?"

"I'm really starting to get tired of this," I answered angrily. It's one thing being humiliated when you know you're slightly in the wrong; but it's something else when you know you're totally in the right. The injustice of it all was galling! "If she doesn't back down, I may seriously have to consider killing her."

"You'd get caught," said Ella. "And either she wouldn't die, or she'd just come back as someone worse."

Enveloped in gloom, Ella came to a stop at her bike.

"All is not lost," I informed her. "I may be down, but I'm not beaten."

"Really?" Ella eyed me curiously. "What's your plan?"

"I'm going to do what I promised." I grinned. "I'm going to tell the truth."

The mood at that afternoon's rehearsal was nervous. Nervous and tense. I exchanged polite greetings with everyone except Carla, but that was as far as conversation went. You could tell the others were all waiting to see what would happened between Princess Santini and me.

I gave away nothing until we were ready to start.

"All right!" boomed Mrs. Baggoli. "Places, everyone!"

"Mrs. Baggoli?" I stepped to the edge of the stage. "Mrs. Baggoli," I said loudly and clearly. "There's something I have to say before we begin."

The expression on Mrs. Baggoli's face was like a sigh.

Opening night was only three days away. She didn't want any interruptions.

"Now what?" asked Mrs. Baggoli.

I held my head up, bathed by the spotlight. "Mrs. Baggoli," I said. "I have a confession to make." My eyes met hers. "A confession and an apology."

Someone made a gagging sound from behind me.

"A confession?" Mrs. Baggoli smiled a little uneasily. "A confession about what?"

"I did a terrible thing, Mrs. Baggoli." I spoke slowly, with dignity, dragging the attention of everyone to me.

"Lola . . ." Mrs. Baggoli laughed a little. "What on earth have you done?"

I took a deep breath, the moral torment I'd been enduring showing in my face. "I borrowed Eliza's dress," I said flatly. "I'm really sorry, but I honestly felt that I had no choice."

"Eliza's dress?" Mrs. Baggoli repeated. "No choice?"

I nodded. "Yes." I shook my head. "No, I really had no choice."

Mrs. Baggoli, to her credit, picked up her line automatically.

"But why?" she asked. "Why would you borrow Eliza's dress?"

You could have heard a feather crash to the floor, the room was so quiet. Even Carla Santini wasn't saying anything under her breath—for a change.

"So I could go to the Sidhartha party," I informed her.

Mrs. Baggoli frowned. "The *Sidhartha* party?"

"But you didn't go to the party," said Henry Higgins. "Carla said—"

I turned to him with a small smile. "I know what Carla said. . . . But it isn't true. Ella and I were at the party." I clasped my hands together, looking beseechingly at Mrs. Baggoli. "It was Sidhartha's last concert," I explained. "I had to go. . . ."

"Oh, please . . . ," Carla groaned. "When are you going to give up, Lola?" she demanded. "No one's interested in your lies anymore. First you lied about being invited to the party, and now you've come up with this ridiculous story about Eliza's dress—"

"But how could you possibly have taken the dress?" Mrs. Baggoli was asking. "The closet's always locked."

"There are ways . . . ," I said vaguely.

"Oh, sure," muttered Carla. "Now you want us to believe you're a lock picker as well as a liar."

Mrs. Baggoli scowled in her direction. "Carla, if you don't mind . . ." She turned back to me. "And where is the dress now?"

"I put it back in the drama room."

Mrs. Baggoli got to her feet. "Well, there's one way of settling this," she said more or less to herself. She marched off out of the room.

Carla took advantage of Mrs. Baggoli's absence to take center stage.

"You really are too much, you know?" she declaimed. "I don't know where you get off, thinking you can manipulate everyone the way you do. Just because we don't come from New York City doesn't mean we're stupid, you know." She glanced around at our fellow actors so they'd understand that she was including them in this.

"You're the one who manipulates everyone," I hissed back. "You treat everybody like they're puppets. Everything you say is a lie."

"Here comes Mrs. Baggoli," said Colonel Pickering. He sounded relieved.

Both Carla and I smiled as Mrs. Baggoli came back in the room.

"Well, the dress is back in the closet," says Mrs. Baggoli. "But in all honesty, Lola, I have to say that it doesn't look as though it's been touched." She sounded relieved, too.

"That's because Stu Wolff had it cleaned." I nearly laughed out loud. At last I had my chance to explain— and to an eager audience. "You see, just as we got there, Ella and I saw Stu Wolff leave the party, and we followed him. It'd been raining all afternoon, so the dress got kind of wet and dirty, and Stu had it cleaned for me." I glanced at Carla out of the corner of my eye. "He said it was the least he could do, seeing as Ella and I practically saved his life."

Mrs. Baggoli's eyes shifted between Carla and me. She wasn't sure what to believe anymore.

"Well, maybe you took the dress and maybe you didn't," she said almost vaguely. "As far as I'm concerned, what's important is that it's where it should be now, and in the condition it came to us in."

"But Mrs. Baggoli!" Why wouldn't anyone ever follow the script I was using? "Mrs. Baggoli, I did take the dress." I pulled at my T-shirt. "See? Stu Wolff gave me this to wear so I wouldn't catch pneumonia."

Mrs. Baggoli sat down with finality. "Lola," said Mrs. Baggoli, "I really don't want to continue this discussion now. We have a lot to do before Friday night."

Carla stepped up behind me. "Sure, he did . . . ," she whined in my ear. "Maybe he gave you his class ring, too."

Colonel Pickering and Henry Higgins chortled softly.

Driven by my righteous sense of indignation, I ignored Mrs. Baggoli and turned on Carla. "He did give it to me!" I shouted. "It's a roadie T-shirt from their last tour. Where else would I get it?"

"You got it where you get all your clothes," shrieked Carla. "In a junk store."

I turned to Henry Higgins, Colonel Pickering, and the Parlor Maid, who were all standing a few steps from Carla and me with their mouths open and their eyes wide.

"You believe me, don't you?" I demanded. "Carla's the one who's lying, not I."

The Parlor Maid looked at Carla, and said nothing. Henry Higgins looked at Mrs. Baggoli, and said nothing. Colonel Pickering looked up at the lights and shrugged. Mrs. Baggoli clapped her hands. "Girls! Please!"

I returned to my argument with Carla. "And anyway," I screamed, "I'd rather have my wardrobe than yours. If you couldn't read you'd never be able to get dressed in the morning."

"Your jealousy is disgusting!" sneered Carla. "You're so pathetic I almost feel sorry for you."

"*You* feel sorry for *me*?" I laughed hollowly. "You're the one who's pathetic. Poor little rich girl who can't stand not to have everything her way. You're not even big enough to admit that Ella and I did go to the party. Because of who *we* are, not because of who our *fathers* are."

"Girls!" Mrs. Baggoli was back on her feet. "Did you hear me?" She appeared at the foot of the stage. "I don't know what's going on with the two of you, but it'll stop outside that door." She pointed to the main entrance. "Am I making myself clear?"

I nodded. I couldn't trust myself to speak. It was all so unfair! Hot tears of self-pity welled in my eyes. But no one noticed.

"I mean it," said Mrs. Baggoli. "All of us have worked very hard for this production. I'm not having it ruined by you two. No more. Do you understand? We've all had enough."

"Have you, Lola?" whispered Carla. "Have you finally had enough?"

* * *

Have you, Lola? . . . *Have you finally had enough?* Carla's words echoed in my mind for the rest of the day.

All through rehearsal, even during Eliza's big show-down with Henry Higgins, I watched the others watching me—the rest of the cast impassive, Mrs. Baggoli frowning critically, Carla looking bored—and thought, *Have you, Lola?* . . . *Have you finally had enough?*

At supper, my mother brought up the play.

"We're all really looking forward to it," said my mother. She smiled at her youngest as they snuffled at their food and kicked each other under the table. "Aren't we, girls?"

"What?" asked Paula, through a mouthful of potato.

Pam lobbed a piece of broccoli at her twin's head. "What's it about?"

"How many times do I have to tell you not to play with your food?" shouted my mother. "Pam, you get down on the floor and pick that up right now."

Have you, Lola? . . . *Have you finally had enough?* asked the voice in my head.

It whispered to me while I did my homework; it hissed at me through the splashing of the shower. *Have you, Lola?* . . . *Have you finally had enough?* . . . *Have you, Lola?* . . . *Have you finally had enough?* . . . *Enough?* . . . *Enough?* . . . *Have you finally had enough?*

I didn't know what the answer was. All I knew was that I had seriously underestimated a couple of things, only one of them being Carla Santini. I hadn't realized what the limits were to what people would believe. The man in the ticket store had believed my improbable— but possible—story of a dying sister. The bus driver had believed my improbable—but possible—story of a sister with a broken foot. The bouncer had believed the improbable—but possible—story of my sudden illness. Ella had believed in the deaths of my father and Elk—both possible but not all that probable. The one story I'd told that was both probable *and* possible was the one that was true. And no one believed it. Not even Mrs. Baggoli. I'd always thought it was possible to control your life, but it seemed that it wasn't. To everyone in Deadwood, there was no way I would ever get into the Sidhartha party, and so I hadn't.

Have you, Lola? . . . Have you finally had enough?

"You know what really gets me?" I said to Ella that night on the phone. "What really gets me is that Sam's right. We could never have won. It's like playing cards with a riverboat gambler. The deck's marked. You couldn't win if you played for the rest of your life."

"What does it matter anymore?" asked Ella.

"What does it matter?" Was this the same girl who only weeks before had been begging me to stay out of Carla's way?

"Well, *we* know we went to the party," said Ella. "*We* know we met Stu Wolff. I mean, that's what really counts, isn't it?"

Have you, Lola? . . . Have you finally had enough?

27

MY WILDERNESS DAYS

From then on, Mrs. Baggoli was cool to the point of frostbite through every rehearsal. She was warm and encouraging to the rest of the cast, but when she spoke to Carla or me, she was like a ringmaster entering the lions' cage, chair first.

The others kept their distance, too—at least from me. Carla Santini made sure that they did.

Mrs. Baggoli may have said that whatever was going on between Carla and me would stop outside the auditorium, but that wasn't what Carla heard. Carla heard, "Escalate this battle into a full-scale war, and take no prisoners."

She stopped talking to me completely again. Whenever I made some comment on the play, Carla would pretend to study her nails. Whenever I tried to strike up a conversation with one of the other actors, she'd cut in—smoothly, effortlessly, smilingly—and ice me out. No one even bothered trying to strike up a conversation with me if Carla was around; it wasn't worth the effort. All someone had to do was ask me the time and she'd swoop down like a vulture on a dead rabbit.

And then, on Wednesday, Carla sailed into rehearsal with her curls shaking and a floodlight smile. The rest of us were all at the front of the auditorium. We all looked warily at one another.

"Mrs. Baggoli," screeched Carla. "Mrs. Baggoli, guess what? You won't believe my news!"

Mrs. Baggoli looked up with an expression on her face that suggested that she was prepared to believe anything. "I'm almost afraid to ask," said Mrs. Baggoli.

Carla laughed. "Oh, no, you're going to love this." She spread out her arms as though about to make an important announcement. She took a deep breath. She was ready to burst with excitement.

"My father wants us to have the cast party at our house!" she shrieked. "Isn't that fantastic? He says he insists!"

I'll bet he did.

The cast party isn't exactly the social event of the year. It's what you would call a symbolic celebration. Usually it's held backstage. We were all supposed to bring in something to eat or drink, and Mrs. Baggoli would contribute the cake.

Mrs. Baggoli was taken by surprise. "Why, Carla," she said. "That's very kind of your father, but it's very short notice—"

"Oh, I know, I know. . . ." Carla wrung her lily-white hands. "He's been so busy that it kind of snuck up on him."

Which meant that she'd only just thought of it. It had taken her a while, but she'd finally come up with the way she could play a supporting part and still be the star.

Mrs. Baggoli looked unsure. "Well . . ."

"And he'll pay for everything, of course," said Carla. She smiled on us happily, Lady Bountiful distributing fresh fruit to the poor. "I've been telling him all about the play, of course, and he says it sounds to him like we all deserve something special."

Still blinking in bewilderment, Mrs. Baggoli appealed to the rest of us. "What does everyone else think?" she asked.

"And don't forget, there's the indoor pool," said Carla. "And, of course, we have so much room that everybody's welcome to bring guests." She quivered with girlish excitement. "Oh, please say yes, Mrs. Baggoli. It'll be so much fun!"

Mrs. Baggoli's eyebrows rose. "Any objections?" she asked.

I had an objection. I had several objections. My first objection was that I didn't want to have the cast party at The Castle Santini. A cast party should be held in the theater, with the smell of greasepaint all around and the roar of the crowd still echoing in your ears. Secondly, I knew Carla well enough to know that with the party at her house, she'd be the one who would act like the star. My third was that I doubted I'd be allowed in. Fourthly, if—through some oversight or minor miracle—I were allowed in, I knew that, somehow, some way, Carla would make sure that I had less fun than a turkey at Thanksgiving. But I didn't say anything. How could I? Carla's cleverness had reached new heights. In spite of all my objections, there was no way I could *not* go without seeming petty and ungrateful. Mrs. Baggoli wouldn't give me so much as a walk-on in the future if I let down the drama club and didn't turn up.

"Well, that's settled then," said Mrs. Baggoli. "Thank your father very much and tell him we'll see him Friday night."

Carla swept her smile by me. "He'll be so happy!" she gushed. "He's really looking forward to it."

I sank into a depression that was deeper than the ocean and just as wide. I'd never before felt so totally defeated, so completely without hope, in my entire life. Not even the dark days when we first moved to Dellwood were this dark. Even if I was fantastic in *Pygmalion*—which, of course, I would be—no one would remember me as Lola Cep, the girl who was Eliza Doolittle. They'd remember me as Lola Cep, the girl who was pathetic.

That night, I lay on my bed, listening to the sounds of daily life emanating from the rest of the house, while the anxiety monsters crawled out of the darkness, thrashing and roaring around me.

I was clawed by self-doubt. Maybe I wasn't as good an actor as I'd thought. Maybe it didn't matter whether I was or I wasn't. Maybe, no matter how pure your passion or true your heart, you can never win against the Carla Santinis of this world.

I slept fitfully, tormented by dreams. It was the night of the play. I was up on-stage, but I was also in the audience. Everyone around me was talking about *me*. But not about my performance; not about the wit and insight I brought to Eliza. "Isn't that the girl who lies?" they were saying. "Isn't that the girl who told everyone that her father was dead so she wouldn't seem so boring?" Every time Carla walked on-stage they cheered. "She should have gotten the part of Eliza," the audience whispered. "They must have given it to that other girl out of pity. Because she's so pathetic."

I woke up suddenly in the middle of the night, my face damp with sweat. I could hear the house groaning and the pipes creaking and the scratching of the pine tree against the front window. But I could hear something else.

Have you, Lola? . . . Have you finally had enough?

By the time I was getting ready for school the next day, I'd made my decision. I wasn't going to be in the play. For the first time in my life, I was giving up. It wasn't just the Santini Big Freeze. It wasn't just the way the rest of the cast avoided me in order to have a quiet life. It wasn't the fed-up way Mrs. Baggoli watched my every move. It wasn't even the fact that Carla had managed to move the party to her house where she could swan around like she was the star. It was the way everyone looked at me—even the kids I knew really liked me—as though I'd just been released from jail for a crime they were sure I'd done.

To answer Carla's question, I'd had enough. She'd beaten me. Not fairly and squarely, maybe, but she'd definitely beaten me. Carla Santini could be Queen of Deadwood forever, for all I cared.

I didn't say anything to anyone, not even Ella. Cataclysmic personal defeat isn't the kind of thing you want to share, not even with your best friend. Like a deer that's been hit by a Land Rover, I just wanted to slink into the forest and die by myself.

In fact, Ella and I didn't talk much that day. I was in too deep a state of grief for idle chitchat, and besides that, I was laying the ground for a sudden attack of influenza. It was the easiest way. I mean, I couldn't very well go to Mrs. Baggoli and say, "I've decided to step down as Eliza, since Carla wants the part so much."

I was quiet and distracted in my classes.

My teachers noticed that the student they relied on for animated participation was listless and withdrawn.

"Lola," they said. "Are you all right? You're very quiet today."

"It's nothing," I answered. "I have a headache," or "My throat's a little sore," or, by the end of the afternoon, "I think I have a fever."

As soon as I got home, I took to my bed.

My mother found me, prostrate on the couch,

wrapped in the old granny-square afghan my dad cro-
cheted when he hurt himself falling off a mountain in
the Catskills and was laid up for a few weeks. Whenever
anyone's sick in Ella's house, they take an aspirin and go
to bed. But whenever anyone's sick in my house, they lie
on the couch with the afghan and watch TV.

"What's wrong?" asked my mother. "Aren't you feeling well?" Her usual suspiciousness had been replaced
with maternal concern. She knew the play meant more
to me than anything; it wouldn't occur to her that I was
only acting.

I raised my head as she crossed the room. "My throat
hurts," I croaked, barely loud enough to be heard. "And
my head . . ." I fell back against the pillows. "I think I
have a fever. . . ." I stifled a moan of pain. "My skin feels
like it's on fire."

My mother wiped her hands on her clay-covered
apron and felt my forehead. Her face clouded with concern. "You do feel warm. . . ."

I should have felt warm; I'd been lying there with the
hot-water bottle pressed to my head, waiting for her to
come out of her studio.

"I hope you're not coming down with something. . . ."

"I'm sure it's nothing," I whispered hoarsely.
"Stress . . ."

"It could be the flu," said my mother. "There's a lot of
it going around. . . ." She started feeling my glands.
"Serves you right for running around in that storm on
Saturday."

"I can't be sick," I moaned feebly. "Tomorrow's *Pygmalion*. I have to be all right for that."

"I'll make you some herbal tea," said my mother, "and a compress for your fever. Maybe it's just one of those twenty-four-hour bugs."

I moaned again. "It has to be," I said as she bustled out of the room. "I can't miss the play."

My mother's voice was respectfully low and full of concern. "I'm really sorry, Ella," she was saying, "but I'm afraid she can't come to the phone. She isn't feeling well."

She paused while Ella spoke.

"It looks like some kind of flu," my mother continued. "You know, throat, head, and fever. But despite all appearances, she isn't going to die. It doesn't look like she'll be going to school tomorrow though."

I could hear the sound of Ella's voice coming through the receiver, but not the words themselves.

"I know," said my mother, "it really is a shame. My folks are coming all the way from Connecticut, and of course, there's Mary's dad. . . . They're all going to be really disappointed."

I didn't want to hear about all the people I was supposedly letting down. I lifted my hand and waved it in my mother's direction. I was much too weak and my voice much too sore to tell her to say hello to Ella for me.

My mother gave me a nod. "She says to say 'hello,'" she said to Ella. My mother looked over at me again. "Ella says 'hi,'" she reported.

"That'd be great," said my mother. "I'll tell her."

"Tell me what?" I asked, as my mother hung up the phone.

"Ella says she'll make sure she gets all your homework for you."

Struggling against the pain, I smiled my gratitude. What a friend.

As you can imagine, I had another bad night. Every time I closed my eyes, I saw Carla Santini in the red satin dress, smiling into the spotlight like a glacier. I heard the cheers and cries of "Bravo!" I watched her step in front of everyone else to take another bow.

I was awake at dawn.

I knew I was doing the right thing; I was sure of it. It meant that I had forever lost the fight against Carla Santini and the forces of darkness, but what did it matter? There's no point in waging a battle you know you'll lose even if you win.

All I had to do was stay in bed for the next twenty-four hours, and it would all be over. But I had to stop thinking about it. I had to stop the corkscrew of pain that gouged at my heart every time I imagined Carla Santini in Eliza's dress.

I heard my mother get up and go into the kitchen. I

heard the twins erupt into consciousness. I heard the radio go on. The weather was going to be mild and sunny. I'd been hoping for rain. Rain's always so comforting when you're unhappy. And then I heard the front bell. I looked at my clock. It was too early for the mailman with a package, or even for the UPS man, come to take some boxes of dinnerware away.

Pam tripped over something and fell, so Paula reached the door first.

"She's sick!" shouted Paula. "She isn't going to school today. So now we don't have to go to her boring play."

"Now nobody has to go to the boring play," said Ella.

This was not Ella-like behavior, this coming to the house at seven-thirty in the morning. She hadn't been able to bring me my homework the afternoon before because she had to do something with her mother at the last minute, but I'd figured she'd wait till the weekend to come. I had the thought to jump up and lock the door, but before I could, it opened and Ella Marjorie Gerard, the girl once destined to be picked as Most Shy in our high-school yearbook, marched in.

"I want to talk to you," said Ella, and she slammed the door in Pam and Paula's faces.

"Not now," I said. I rubbed my eyes sleepily. "I just woke up."

Ella threw her book bag on the foot of my bed. "Oh, sure you did," said Ella.

"I really don't feel well—" I began.

"You can cut the crap," said the most polite and well-mannered teenager in New Jersey. "I know what you're doing." She grabbed the blanket and yanked it off me. "And I'm not going to let you get away with it. Get up now and get dressed for school."

I stared at her, agog. I'd never heard Ella talk to anyone like that. I didn't think she was capable of it.

"I'm telling you I'm sick," I said. I pulled the blanket back around me, shivering slightly. "I have a fever," I told her. "Ask my mother."

"What do you think I am, stupid?" asked Ella. "You're not sick. You're bailing out of the play." She folded her arms in front of her and set her jaw. She looked like she was in a play herself. "You're giving up," said Ella.

Admitting defeat was getting easier and easier.

"All right," I snapped. "So what if I am?" I glared at her. "I wish I'd done it when you wanted me to. I could have saved myself a lot of time and trouble."

"Well, I don't want you to now," said Ella. She dropped her arms and sat down on the bed. "You can't do this, Lola. Everybody's depending on you."

Sure they were. Depending on me to play the fool.

"Hah hah," I said. "Nobody will even notice the difference."

"Of course they will," said Ella. "What about your parents? And your grandparents? And me? And Sam? Sam's never been to a school function before in his life. He's only going for you."

"Maybe he can get a refund." I fluffed up my pillow and leaned back. "Maybe all of you can."

"I can't believe I'm hearing this," said Ella. "This isn't like you at all. What happened to the person who never gives up? What happened to the person who told me her motto was 'never say die'?"

"I don't know," I said. Which was true. "I guess she bailed out, too."

Ella gazed at me in silence for several seconds.

"So that's it?" she said at last. "All that stuff you told me about passion and art and putting your work before yourself, that was just more of your lies?"

"Of course not," I said. "That's what's important. It's just that I—"

"You're just the same as Carla, aren't you?" Ella stood up. "It's all me, me, me, and I, I, I. Nobody else counts for anything, do they?"

I stood up, too.

"That's not true and you know it!" I felt like I was falling apart inside.

"No, I don't know it!" Ella screamed back. "You haven't given one thought to anybody else in all this. It's all been about you." She flung her arms wide, appealing to the gods themselves. "What about me?" she demanded. "I was miserable until you came to Dellwood. Totally miserable. I thought that everybody's life was like mine, just doing all the things you're sup-posed to do when you're supposed to do them, and never questioning anything. I thought that when I grew up, all I could expect was a life like my parents'." She was trembling with rage. "And then I met you. You gave me courage, Lola. You taught me that you can make life what you want."

I reached out to touch her shoulder. I'd never seen Ella cry before. "Ella, I—"

She jumped back as though I'd threatened her with a saber. "Don't touch me!" She wiped her eyes with the sleeve of her shirt. "You're a sham, Lola Cep; that's what you are. I thought being the best Eliza Doolittle you could be was what mattered to you. But it isn't. Because if it was, you'd go on tonight and you'd be the best Eliza Doolittle, no matter what Carla Santini says or does." Ella's face was red and blotchy from crying. "Don't you get it, Lola? That's the one thing she can't do anything about. The one thing nobody can do anything about! And you're just going to hand it to her."

By now, I was crying, too.

"What's going on in there?" called my mother. She started banging on the door. "Mary? Ella?"

I snuffed back a few million tears. "Nothing," I shouted back through my sobs. "I've had a miraculous recovery."

28

NEVER SAY DIE

Henry Higgins and I peered through the curtain at the side of the stage.

On the left of the auditorium were Mr. and Mrs. Gerard, Ella, and Sam. Mr. and Mrs. Gerard were both wearing suits; Ella was wearing the A-line with the pearl buttons down the front she'd wanted me to wear to the party, but it didn't look so bad because her hair was loose, and the contrast between the copper and the blue was actually stunning; and Sam was wearing black jeans and a black T-shirt and his leather jacket with the bottle caps bolted to it. They looked so out of place together that a passing policeman would have arrested Sam for holding the Gerards hostage.

On the right-hand side were my mother and father, the twins, my grandparents, and about a dozen of my mother's closest friends. My parents were sitting together, with a twin on either side, to keep them from talking during the performance.

"Corblighme," whispered Henry Higgins in a mid-Atlantic drawl. "It's a full house. There are even people standing at the back."

I was too excited to comment on his hopeless accent,

but I will say that it was just as well that Mrs. Baggoli moved the play to America.

"Henry! Eliza!"

We jumped back. Mrs. Baggoli has a stage whisper that makes the floorboards quake.

"Get in your places!" hissed Mrs. Baggoli. "Three minutes till curtain!"

Henry Higgins took his place by the supermarket painted on the backdrop. I took up my place in the wings with my groceries.

Everybody started telling everybody else to break a leg, the way actors do.

"Break a leg!"

"Break a leg!"

"Break a leg!"

I looked over at Carla Santini. It is a testament to my renewed determination and resolution that I didn't say, "Break a neck!" I thought it, but I didn't say it. I am above such childish pettiness. I will never sink to her level again; I don't like being down that low.

"Good luck, everyone!" boomed Mrs. Baggoli, as she skittered into the wings. "Give them a show they won't forget!"

I was scared, I'll admit it. Now that the play was actually about to begin, panic and doubt began marching around in my heart. What if I wasn't any good after all? What if Carla managed to sabotage me with just a whisper or a smile?

"Never say die," I said to myself. "Never say die."

I pictured the faces of the Ceps, the Gerards, the Kapoks, and the solitary Creek—the Gerards with their hands folded neatly on their laps, the Ceps and Kapoks pushing and slapping and shoving each other, and the Creek unwrapping a stick of gum. It was going to be all right. I would play to them. I wanted them to be proud of me. All of them, even Mr. and Mrs. Gerard. Even Pam and Paula. But especially Ella.

It was a triumph!

We had ten curtain calls and a standing ovation. I was dizzy from bowing so much.

Mrs. Baggoli came on-stage for the last curtain call, passing out a single rose to every member of the cast. When she was done, she put an arm around me and one around Henry Higgins. "My stars!" she cried to the audience. She squeezed my shoulder.

Sam and Ella came backstage.

"You were wonderful!" screeched Ella. "Even my parents think so. My mom said she totally forgot it was you up there."

Sam grinned. "Not bad," he said. "That's my first play, not counting the story of the first Christmas in kindergarten."

Heedless of the makeup I was smearing all over her face, I gave Ella a hug. "Thanks," I whispered.

"We'll wait for you outside," said Ella. "Sam's going to drive us to the party."

"I've bet Ella that the Santinis' butler won't let me in," said Sam.

I tossed my hair and flashed my teeth in a Carla Santini way. "All you have to do is say you're with me," I crowed. "I'm the star!"

"Lola Cep!" Mrs. Baggoli clapped her hands. "Mrs. Ludley wants to lock up. Get out of your costume!"

At least my success hadn't spoiled Mrs. Baggoli.

"I'm going," I said. "I won't be five minutes."

The only other person in our changing room (the girls' restroom) was Carla Santini. She was leaning over a sink, redoing her face for off-stage life.

"Congratulations," said Carla, her eyes on me in the mirror. "You're a big hit."

Such generosity demanded generosity in return. "Thanks," I said, stepping up to the sink beside her. "We're all a big hit."

Carla tossed her lip gloss into her make-up bag. For once, she wasn't smiling. "I have to hand it to you, Lola," she said. "There's more to you than I thought."

"To you, too," I said with total sincerity. "Much more."

Carla laughed. A rueful expression appeared on her face.

"What couldn't we do if we worked together?" she mused. "You know, sometimes I almost think it's a shame that you and I aren't in the same club."

"You've got to be kidding," I said to her reflection. "I couldn't afford to belong to any club you were in."

Carla laughed again. I guess she took it as a compliment.

266